CRUISING

CRUISING
GAY EROTIC STORIES

EDITED BY
SHANE ALLISON

CLEiS
PRESS

Published in the United States by Cleis Press Inc., 2246 Sixth Street, Berkeley, California 94710.

Printed in the United States.
Cover design: Scott Idleman/Blink
Cover photograph: Damir Spanic/Getty Images
Text design: Frank Wiedemann
First Edition.
10 9 8 7 6 5 4 3 2 1

Trade paper ISBN: 978-1-57344-786-7
E-book ISBN: 978-1-57344-799-7

"Francois at the *Toilette*," © copyright 2011 by Gerard Wozek, was previously published on Velvet Mafia. "Jonah and the Whale," by Aaron Travis, was previously published in *Friction* magazine (June, 1987). "School Queer," by Bob Vickery, was previously published in *Friction 5*, edited by Jesse Grant and Austin Foxxe (Alyson Publications, 2003). "Three Weeks in the Cemetery," by Shaun Levin, was previously published in a very different form in *Afterwords: Real Sex from Gay Men's Diaries*, edited by Kevin Bentley (Alyson Publications, 2001).

Contents

INTRODUCTION

I was walking toward the Bellamy Building bathroom when I noticed the white boy brunet. He was kind of thick, sporting a black T-shirt and a pair of red basketball shorts; the kind with the material that shows off a deep impression of the dick. I like them better than sweatpants, where you can only see a bulge, but these shorts show everything. He wasn't hard from what I could tell. His dick just hung pressed against the maroon polyester athletic material. I don't think he was wearing any underwear. I wanted to reach out and cop a feel of his package, but I dared not if I didn't want to be belted in the mouth for making such a bold move. Needless to say, his teasing tool was all I needed to put me in a prime mood for cruising. The imprint of this college boy's johnson was kicking against my naughty brain.

It's hard to believe that after countless years of hot sexual tearoom experiences, I am still cruising for it well into my thirties. I was very young when I began; it all started innocently enough, if you call standing at the pissers in the bathroom of

Parkway 5 taking a peek at the dicks of anonymous men an act of innocence. As I sit here writing this, I'm thinking of the men I encountered during my earlier heyday of cruising, wondering how they are, what they're doing, if they've found new stomping grounds in which to tap their feet for blow jobs. I've seen a few of them about town, in bookstores, the mall, movie theaters. They act like they don't remember me, and perhaps they don't. We don't call each other out, fully aware of the unspoken, anonymous oath between us. I wish every single one of them well wherever they might be.

Some of you might be wondering why I didn't find a safer, less risky way to meet men, and what I can say is, if you didn't grow up in the "gayorotti" like New York or San Francisco, but had to endure being black and gay in a small town, meeting men is anything but a cakewalk. Growing up, I didn't know what a gay club, a gay bookstore or a GLBT community center was. I didn't know to seek these places out until I was nineteen. Just about every sexual experience I had started in a bathroom stall. Even the first time I kissed a boy happened behind the mustard-yellow walls of a school bathroom. By the time I was fourteen, it was all I knew. It wasn't like I could go around the halls of my high school grabbing the butts of boys I deemed cute or ask that boy I was crushing on to go to the prom with me, like my privileged hetero counterparts. No, instead of having a girlfriend to help me curb my insatiable appetite for sex, I had to settle for jack-off sessions in a mall bathroom.

By the time I reached my twenties and was in college, I was tapping my feet for a salacious good time. But don't feel sorry for me; don't get all sad and mushy, because I've had some of the hottest sex in bathroom stalls and the booths of sex arcades. Let's see—how can I explain it? I love the rush that washes over me when I cruise. It's that feeling I get right here in the pit of my stomach moments before I shove that proverbial bathroom door open. It's about that sensation of arousal at the sight of a guy's underwear down around his knees or what is shoved forth to me through a sand-dollar-sized glory hole. Even the rush of getting popped by a cop is enough to shoot my loins over the moon, or in this anthology's case, the partition.

This is the anthology I have always wanted to do. When I initially came up with the idea for it, I sought to find those of like mind who had experienced that rush identical to my own, and oh, man, did I find them. If you want to know where the action is, you're sure to find plenty of it in the pages of these seventeen stories promising to titillate, inspire and get your rocks off, guys, so please enjoy.

Shane Allison
Tallahassee, Florida

SCHOOL QUEER

Bob Vickery

Saturday night is my night to shine. All the guys neck with their dates out at Bass Lake or the drive-in over on Route 27, or maybe at Jackson Lookout, but because the girls here are all "saving themselves," they wind the guys up so tight that these boys could fuck a knotty pine by the time they finally take the little virgins home. So with blue balls aching, they head out to the back of the Bass Lake boathouse, where they know they'll find me waiting. I suck the hard cocks of these Southern Baptist boys, letting them frantically fuck my face, their eyes shut tight, imagining it's not my lips wrapped around their stiff, urgent dicks, but *pussy*. So they groan, their full-to-bursting balls slapping against my chin, and when they finally shoot, they cry out "Cindy Lou" or "Peggy Beth" as their loads splatter against the back of my throat. When they've finally got the relief they've been denied all evening, the guys pull up their jeans and walk away, disappearing into the bushes without so much as a "Thanks." Before I can get too resentful, the next shadowy figure rounds the corner of the boathouse, and the ritual starts up all over again. Sometimes there are actual lines, or else the guys stand side by side, and I go down the row and work the stiff dicks that are throbbing in front of me. During the week, I'm shunned by nearly everyone on the campus of this small Baptist school, but on Saturday night they can't get enough of me. It's a lonely life, being the school queer, but I serve a useful function, and so I'm tolerated.

I don't suck every dick that's offered to me. And of the men I do suck off, I do have my favorites. Bill McPherson tops the list. What a sweet, hot guy. I can tell that he was raised right: well-nourished, muscular body; straight teeth; clear complexion; glossy, brown hair; steady blue eyes that meet your gaze with honest conviction. And so *earnest!* That's the charm of these Baptist boys. They're so damn *wholesome*; you just want to eat them up. Bill is well liked about the campus, an unexceptional student but still a big fish in this tiny pond: captain of the wrestling team and vice-president of the Kappa Gamma Chi fraternity. And he dates Becky Michaelson, this year's Azalea Princess in the school's Homecoming Parade, who, lucky for me, holds on to her cherry as if it were a piece of the One True Cross. More Saturdays then I can remember, Bill has come around behind the boathouse, frustrated, shy, embarrassed; dropped his pants and offered up his dick to me. And it's such a beautiful dick: thick, meaty, veined, pink and swollen, with a head that flares out like a fleshy, red plum. I love making love to Bill's dick. I suck it slowly, drag my tongue up the shaft and then around the head, probing into Bill's piss slit, working my lips down the thick tube of flesh, rolling Bill's ball sac around in my mouth as I stroke him, drawing Bill to the brink of shooting, backing off, and then drawing him even closer. Bill gasps and groans, his breathing gets heavy, his body trembles under my hands as I knead and pull on his muscled torso, and when he finally shoots, he cries out "Sweet Jesus in Heaven!" every time, like he's offering his orgasm to God. When I finally climb to my feet, wiping my mouth, damn if Bill doesn't look me in the eye, shake my hand and thank me. It's a small thing, maybe, but he's the only one who does that, and that gives me just one more reason to like him.

Except for his final thanks, Bill has never spoken to me during our cocksucking sessions, so it's something of a surprise when one summer night, while I'm on my knees before him, he clears his throat and asks, "Do...do you ever do this to Nick Stavros?"

I take Bill's dick out of my mouth and look up at him, but his face is in shadow and I can't read his expression. I know from seeing the two of them around campus together that Bill and Nick are good friends. "Yeah," I say. "Nick comes around here from time to time. Not nearly as much as you do."

Bill doesn't say anything, and I pick up where I left off. I twist my head as I slide my lips up Bill's shaft, because I know Bill likes that. Bill starts pumping his hips, sliding his dick in and out of my mouth. After a minute of this, Bill clears his throat again. "What's Nick's dick like?" he asks. I look up at him again, and Bill, seeing the questioning expression on my face, laughs nervously. "Nick's always kidding me about what a ladies' man he is," he says, "and so I was just curious about how he...well, measures up to me."

"You don't have anything to worry about," I say. "Your dick is awesome." I put it back in my mouth.

"Yeah, well, okay," Bill says. "But what's Nick's dick like?"

This is weird, I think. "You really want me to describe Nick's dick?"

"Yeah," Bill says. "Do you mind?" By his tone of voice I'm almost sure he's blushing.

"Unlike yours, it's uncut," I say, "and a lot darker. It curves down, which makes it easier for me to suck, though I sometimes wonder if that would make it harder for him to actually fuck someone. It's a mouthful, but not quite as long as yours, though maybe a little thicker. His piss slit is really pronounced."

Bill is listening to me intently, as if there's going to be an after-lecture test on all of this. I half expect him to start taking notes. When he doesn't say anything else, I return to blowing him. After a minute of this he clears his throat again. "And his balls, what are they like?"

Okaaay, I think. "He's got some low-hangers," I say. "They're a couple of bull-nuts. When he fucks my face, they slap against my chin. I love sucking on them, washing them with my tongue, though I can only do them one at a time. They're too big for them both to fit in my mouth at the same time."

Bill says nothing else for the rest of my blow job. As his dick gets harder, right before he shoots, he runs his fingers through my hair and tugs at it. "Sweet Jesus in Heaven" he murmurs, as usual, and then I feel his dick pulse and soon my mouth is flooded with his load. I stay like that for a long moment, on my knees before Bill, his dick slowly softening in my mouth. Finally, he pulls out and pulls his jeans up. As always, he shakes my hand and thanks me before disappearing into the night.

From that night on, we settle into a new routine. Whenever I suck Bill off, he peppers me with questions, asking for more details on Nick's cock, or his balls, or what his ass is like; how he acts when he shoots. And I answer every question, describing in detail just what it feels like to have Nick slide his dick in my mouth; how Nick likes to push my face hard against his belly, me choking on his dick, my nose pressed against his crinkly, black pubes. Or what Nick's balls smell like, the sweaty, pungent scent of a male animal in rut. Or the low grunts Nick gives as his load squirts down my throat, and what that load tastes like (salty, with just a faint undertaste of garlic). And I feel Bill's dick stiffen with each description I give of Nick, and I think how strange it is to know Bill's secret: just how queer he is for Nick.

One day Bill catches up to me on the campus green. I try to hide my surprise. Normally nobody as high up on the campus pecking order as Bill would be caught dead talking in public to the school queer.

"Hey, Pete," he says. "How's it going?"

"I'm okay," I say cautiously.

We walk along the brick path in silence. The people we pass stare at us with the same astonishment that I feel. "Look, Pete," Bill says, lowering his voice but keeping his eyes straight ahead. "Can you be at the boathouse tonight? Around eleven?"

I let a couple of beats go by. "It's a weekday night, Bill. I have a chemistry test tomorrow that I have to study for."

Bill stops and looks at me, and I can see the desperation in his eyes. "I'm begging you, man," he says.

This is all *very* weird. "Okay," I finally say. "If it's that big a deal for you, I'll be there."

Bill looks relieved. "Thanks," he says, and then turns on his heel and walks off.

The moon is nearly full tonight, and its light bounces off the lake and flickers onto the boathouse walls. I sit on one of the overturned boats, smoking a cigarette, waiting. I glance at my watch: five after eleven. There's a rustle of bushes, and then Bill steps out into the light.

"Hi, Bill," I say. But Bill is looking behind him, not toward me. The bushes rustle again, and suddenly Nick walks out and stands next to Bill. He looks at me, scowling, and then looks away.

Bill takes a couple of steps closer. "Nick and I were double dating tonight," he says, "but our girls just wouldn't put out." He gives a laugh that rings as false as a tin nickel. "And boy do we have a nut to bust! So we just swung by here tonight on the off chance that you'd be here to help us get a little relief."

I look at Nick, but he's still staring at the ground, refusing to meet my eye. My gaze shifts back to Bill. "You guys are in luck," I say dryly. "I'm normally not here on a weekday night."

Neither Bill nor Nick says anything. After a couple of beats, I guess that it's up to me to get this ball rolling. "Who wants to go first?" I ask.

"Why don't you go ahead, Nick?" Bill says, turning toward him. "I'll wait."

Nick shrugs, still not saying anything. He's wearing a school T-shirt that hugs his torso, and a pair of cutoffs. Nick can be a surly bastard, and I like Bill way better, but there's no denying he's the handsomer of the two: intense, dark eyes; an expressive mouth; powerful arms; a muscle-packed torso; tight hips... As always, I feel my heart racing as he unbuckles his belt. I pull his cutoffs down past his thighs, and his fleshy, half-hard dick swings heavily from side to side.

"You take care of my buddy, Pete," Bill says. "Suck him good!"

I glance at Bill. His lips are parted and there's a manic gleam in his eyes. If he were any more excited, he'd have a stroke. Because I like Bill, I decide to give him the show he so obviously wants. I look up at Nick. "Why don't you take off all your clothes?" I say quietly. "It'll be more fun that way."

Nick glares down at me. After a brief pause, he hooks his fingers under the edge of his T-shirt and pulls it over his head, revealing his muscularly lean torso. He kicks off his shoes and steps out of his cutoffs. "Okay?" he asks sarcastically. I glance again at Bill. He's looking at Nick's naked body like a starving dog eyeing a T-bone steak.

"Yeah," I say. "That's just fine." I wrap my hand around Nick's dick and give it a squeeze. A clear drop of precome oozes out of his piss slit, and I lean forward and lap it up. I roll my tongue around his cockhead and then slide my lips down his shaft. I can feel the thick tube of flesh harden in my mouth to full stiffness. I begin bobbing my head, turning at an angle to give Bill a maximum view of the show. Nick responds by pressing his palms against both sides of my head and pumping his hips, sliding his dick deep down my throat and then pulling out again. Nick always was an aggressive mouth-fucker.

Bill walks up and stands next to Nick. He unzips his jeans and tugs them down, and his dick springs up, fully hard. "Now me," he says hoarsely. I look up into his face, but his eyes are trained on Nick's spit-slicked, fully hard cock. Bill's the big man on campus, and I may be the queer boy with zero status, but tonight the tables are turned. It's clear that ol' Bill would like nothing more than to trade places with me; get down on his knees and work Nick's dick like I'm doing, swallow it, have Nick plow his face. But it'll never happen. The closest he can let himself get to this fantasy is to have me suck his dick with the taste of Nick's dick still in my mouth. I actually pity the guy as I take his dick in my hand and slide my lips down its shaft.

While I work on Bill's dick I reach over and start jacking off Nick. Nick pumps his hips, fucking my fist the same way he fucked my mouth a minute ago. One thrust catches him off balance, and he reaches out and lays his hand on Bill's shoulder to steady him. Bill reacts as if Nick's touch is a jolt of high-voltage current; his body jerks suddenly, and his muscles spasm. *This poor guy wants it so bad,* I think. With my hand still around Nick's dick, I pull him closer to me until his dick is touching Bill's. I open my lips wider and take both their dicks in my mouth, feeling them rub and thrust against each other. Bill trembles with the feel of Nick's dick against his, and Nick's breath comes out in short grunts. I wrap my hands around their ball sacs and give them a good tug. Bill groans, I feel his dick throb, and my mouth is suddenly flooded with his creamy load. "Sweet Jesus in Heaven!" he gasps. Nick thrusts hard down my throat, his breath coming out faster now, his legs trembling. Suddenly his body spasms and his dick squirts too. I suck hard on the two dicks as they pulse in my mouth, their combined loads splattering against the back of my throat. I roll my tongue over the sperm deposits in my mouth, tasting them like a gourmet, mingling the flavors together, savoring them.

Nick and Bill pull away, and there's this brief moment in time where the three of us are frozen in our positions: me still on my knees, come dribbling out of the corners of my mouth, Bill and Nick on either side of me, buck naked, their dicks half hard and sinking fast, their eyes not meeting.

Bill is the first to break the silence. "Damn," he says his voice low. I look up into his eyes, and then the strangest thing happens, for an instant there's a spark, a little jolt of, I don't know...*connection*. For that brief flicker of time, I'm not the school faggot and he's not the big man on campus, we're both buddies who've shared the pleasure of Nick's flesh. Nick pulls up his pants, and this sudden movement breaks the spell. He picks up his T-shirt from the ground and puts it on. "Let's go," he grunts to Bill. He walks back into the bushes and disappears without looking back at either one of us. Bill gets dressed hurriedly and rushes after him. Before he too disappears into the night, he turns and gives me one last look and then plunges into the bushes after Nick.

I get up and smooth my clothes out, take a comb out of my back pocket and comb my hair. I walk in the opposite direction, down to where my car is parked. I'm sure I'll see Bill again this Saturday night, with or without Nick. If he's alone, we'll have something to talk about. Either way, it should be fun.

KEEPER

Jeff Mann

As soon as I spot him across the diner, I know I'm in trouble. Sure, I've seen photos of him during my research, but in person the guy's downright adorable. Dangerously so. I don't want to do this. I know what his fate's likely to be. But hooking him is my job, so I clear my throat, cross the room, shuck off my backpack and jacket and slide into his window booth.

He looks up, startled. The expression on his face changes fast, from annoyed surprise to childlike fascination. He likes the way I look. We've studied him enough to expect that. His name's Jason Dean. He's thirty, a decade younger than I. He's from Georgia; he's been an independent trucker for five years. He's gay, albeit closeted, with a preference for big, furry, dominant men. I've been chosen to appeal to him. Right now, even before we speak, he's hungrily absorbing my shaved head and thick black beard, the swell of muscles beneath my sweatshirt, the chest hair curling over my collar.

"My guess is there aren't a lot of folks in here who know

what that means," I say, pointing to his inner forearm, the bear paw tattoo there. "My name's Buck." I extend my hand.

"H-hey!" stammers my prey. "I-I'm Jason."

We shake. His grip's strong. I'm sharply aware that, as much as I know about him, this is the first time we've touched.

"What do you think it means?" Jason asks with a nervous smile. He looks like a fawn who's spotted movement in the forest and is right on the edge of bolting. "My tattoo?"

The guy's clearly used to caution. Makes sense in the world of cross-country trucking. He'd probably get his ass kicked or lose his job if he were openly into men.

"Means you're a bear who likes bears," I say. "Like me."

I've corralled many a mark in this business, but this is the first one I badly want to bed. The others have been middle-aged, dumpy and dumb. They deserved what they got. This one... already something hard and sharp in me is melting.

"Am I right?" I take up his coffee cup, take a long sip and look him in the eyes.

"Yep." Jason blushes, dropping his gaze. So bashful. So delectable.

"You're one good-looking cub. Want some company? I could do with a hot meal." Beneath the table, I brush his boot with mine.

Jason looks up at me and grins. "Wow. You ain't shy. My lucky day. Sure, man. Meal's on me. Try the SOS—shit on a shingle. Creamed chipped beef, y'know? Best in West Virginia. I got a big helping coming. Or the country-fried steak. Top-notch!"

I've got him now. Thing is, he's kind of got me. He might not be the only one in danger.

We study each other as we eat, as we exchange backgrounds (mine carefully edited). He's about my height, six one, with a baby face so youthful and endearing it's hard not to stroke his cheek. Or warn him. He's relaxing a little now, giving boyish laughs, digging into his meal. I can tell he's excited. Getting turned on by what he thinks is to come. In the dark beneath the table, his foot rubs my calves with greater and greater frequency. Under thick eyebrows his green eyes glow every time he looks at me; it's pretty clear that my desire for him is entirely matched by his desire for me.

I keep smiling, but my heart sinks. I look away, out at violet twilight, January's snow flurries gusting around the parking lot. I think of that warehouse out in the middle of nowhere, how dark it will be there and in the woods out back, where we dug a new hole.

When I look back, I drink in Jason's heat like I do this truck-stop coffee: his wavy brown hair, thick sideburns grading into several days' worth of stubble; the big silver hoops in his ears; full lips curved in a pink bow, almost feminine; his funny little beard—clean-shaven upper lip, neatly trimmed brown goatee covering his chin. The kid looks like a cross between a cowboy and a lumberjack, with his tight jeans, sharp-toed boots, and gray-plaid flannel shirt. It's half open, revealing a red under-shirt that, partly unbuttoned, exposes silver necklaces, one with a cross, and allows me tasty peeks of his brown chest fuzz. His shirtsleeves are rolled up, showing off sinewy biceps. He's intoxicating.

We finish up our pies—coconut cream for him, pecan for me. Dusk's moved into nightfall; the flurries have turned into a light drizzle spotting the window. Beyond the parking lot's glow, I can make out patchy snowbanks, fog capping the hills.

We argue awhile, as men will, about who'll handle the bill. Jason insists, leaving cash on the table. We pull on our jackets— mine black leather, his fleece-lined denim; I grab my backpack, heavy with essentials; we step outside into the night, beneath the porch roof's shelter. Rain pings on the metal above. Jason cocks his tan cowboy hat over his brow, shuffling his feet. "Damn! Cold!" he says, wrapping his arms around himself. "Well, look, Buck, it was so cool to meet you. I, uh, maybe I could get your number? I, I'd like—"

Jesus, now he's timid again. "How about you show me your truck?" I say. "Unless you need to get on the road."

"Sure. Got to get to Chicago tomorrow, but...I was just gonna spend tonight here, in the sleeper. Come on." Jason gives my shoulder a soft slap and heads into the drizzle. I follow, mesmerized by the movement of his round little ass.

"Oh, god, it's been so long!" Jason pants around my cockhead before deep-throating me. He's on his knees in the truck cab, gripping my thighs. Unzipped, I lean back against the passenger seat, stroking his sideburns as he sucks and slurps. The guy's giving me the tightest, sloppiest, most passionate blow job of my life. Something to be said for shy, sex-starved country boys: their hunger makes them at the least wildly eager, at the most superbly skillful.

Rain's pounding the roof, streaming down the windshield. In the dim light, I check my wristwatch. Got about fifteen minutes before I'm expected to call in and report on my progress. "Let's see your chest," I say.

"You bet, man! I love my nips played with!" In a rush, Jason unbuttons his shirt, tears it off, then unbuttons his undershirt to the waist. "Would you do that? Please? Play with my nips? Kinda rough?"

He's so desperate to be touched, so keen to please. Before I can answer, his lips are wrapped around my dick again, his tongue ranging up and down the shaft. I chuckle, wiping slobber off his chin. "Sure, buddy." Reaching inside his undershirt, I caress his chest—it feels flaming hot contrasted to the cold air of the cab—tug at the hair over his breastbone, find the hard points of his nipples. As soon as I begin a soft massaging, Jason stiffens, moans around my cock, and sucks even more frantically. The harder I work his tits, the harder he sucks, his head bobbing in my lap. He unzips his jeans, pulls out his own cock and jacks himself.

"Umm, you taste so good!" he mumbles. Inside his talented mouth, his throat's tight sheath, I can feel delight building, release looming. "Easy, easy," I say. "I don't want to cum yet. Get up here. You do kiss, don't you?"

"Hell, yes!" Immediately he clambers up into the seat. We kiss, long and deep, his arms wrapped around me so tight you'd think I were driftwood and he were drowning.

"Please, Buck?" Jason whispers. "Please, would you...would you...ride me? Been so long. I need it bad. I need...I need a big man like you...inside me."

"You bet," I say.

"Come on back," Jason says, tugging my hand. "In the sleeper."

I grab my backpack and follow him in. He turns on a lamp. It's a tiny space, with a bed just big enough for two if those two slept close. We fall across it, kissing and grappling. I tug at his undershirt, trying to pull it from his pants. It resists.

"It's, uh, one piece." Jason says, sheepish.

I laugh. "A union suit? I haven't seen one of those since I was a kid. You really *are* country."

"Hey! You seem to savor my country! It's Carhartt. Keeps me warm during long winter hauls."

"Very hot. Bet you'll be even hotter out of it." I sit back, give him a grin and a shove. "Strip, boy." As much of a bottom as he seems to be, the word "boy" should ramp him up even more.

"Yes, *sir!*" Jason grins. Yep, I was right.

While he's hopping around, pulling off boots, jeans, union suit, I'm checking my watch and studying his body as it's revealed—delicious sight of his curvy asscheeks and brown hair in the cleft between. I'm unzipping my backpack, fetching what I need. Now he turns to me, naked save for boot socks. He's just fucking beautiful, with that winter-pale skin; that strong torso and flat belly dusted with hair; those hard, lean arms; those slim hips; that short, fat cock rising between thick, hairy thighs. He turns to me, smiling, so full of hope and trust it's heartbreaking, so eager to give himself, only to find me holding a gun.

Jason gives a little squeak, like a rusty door closing. He stands there, staring at me, pretty lips half parted, dick stiff. He rubs his knuckles across his eyes—right hand, then left—as if he could erase the facts and change his vision. The smile erodes slowly, not all at once.

"Sit down," I say.

He does immediately, on the far end of the bed. He sits stiffly, hands clasped over his crotch.

"No, this is not part of some sex scene, kid. I'm hijacking this truck." I lift the balled-up bandana. "Take this."

Jason hesitates, looks at the pistol in my hand, and obeys.

"Do you know what you're hauling back there?"

"Sure! It's—"

"Not what's obvious. What's hidden."

His eyebrows arch. His eyes widen. Such a pretty green. Long lashes like a girl's.

"You're paid not to know. Right? Not to ask questions?"

Jason nods. Hugging himself, he stares at the floor.

"Cram that rag in your mouth."

He lifts his head. His lips pucker and tremble.

"P-please, man! P-please, no." His voice rises and cracks. "Don't hurt me. I ain't done nothing to you."

"Do what I say, and maybe you'll get through this."

"W-what, what you gonna do with me?"

"Shut up, cowboy." Why is it so hard to be stern with him? The others, it was so easy not to care, to look at them and see nothing but an inconvenience, an obstacle between me and a fine haul. "You do what I say, and maybe I'll protect you from my friends."

"F-f-friends?" Jason stutters. Poor kid's so terrified he's about to piss himself. He'd be even more afraid if he knew the fate of his predecessors.

"Yes, friends. Quite a few of them. All mean as snakes. I need to call them really soon. So get to it, or I'll pistol-whip you."

Jason stuffs the bandana in his mouth. His cheeks bulge.

Pure aphrodisiac, his fear and submission. My cock's throbbing. "All the way in. Good boy. Now this." I toss him the roll of duct tape. "Over your mouth, around your head three or four times." Within a minute, he's gagged himself good and tight, and I'm so hard it hurts. He stares at me, whimpering. I study his baby face, the impression his lips make against the shiny tape. Tears well up in his eyes and spill over. Shamefaced, he bows his head.

"Good. Now these." I lift the cuffs. "Behind your back."

Jason locks the metal around one wrist, puts his hands behind him, fumbles a little. A tiny click and he's helpless. Another few minutes, and I've restrained him so tightly and so thoroughly there's no hope of escape: yards of rope knotted around his ankles, around his knees, around his chest both above and below his nipples, and around his elbows and biceps, imprisoning his arms against his sides.

"There we go," I say, patting his head. "All done."

My captive sits on the bed, chest heaving. He's quite a picture, silver cross glinting in his brown chest hair, tape silvery against his stubbly face, taut rope trussing his wiry frame. He looks up at me with wild eyes, then bows his head and begins sobbing softy. I should shove him into a corner, tell him to buck up, shut up, but instead I sit beside him and wrap my arms around him. I kiss his plump cheek, his taped lips. He resists me at first, squirming around, muscles straining against his bonds. Soon he stops struggling. He slumps against me, trembling violently, and cries harder.

"Easy, kid, easy. You cold?" When he nods, I lower him onto his back on the bed and cover him with blankets. I wipe the tears from his face; he blinks up at me, breathing hard through his nose. Slowly his weeping subsides.

He's so, so scared. I stroke his tousled hair, kiss his brow again and again. Pity pools inside me, mingling with arousal. What am I doing? I'm treating him like my lover, not my captive, not the fool destined for that hole in the forest floor. "You're going to keep still and be quiet, right? Be a good boy?"

Nodding, he closes his eyes. I flip open my phone and make the call.

My burly compatriot Ken drives, listening to country music, smoking one cigarette after another. The truck thrums around us; snow-quilted pastures pour by. We're far from the Flatwoods truck stop now, deep in the countryside of Braxton County. Another half an hour, and we'll reach the warehouse where the others wait.

"I'm going to watch the captive, okay? Let me know when we get there."

"Sure." Ken grins, blowing out smoke. "I'm sure he bears watching. Looks like a real dangerous dude."

"Absolutely." I chuckle. We've worked together for a few years now; Ken gets me. He figured out long ago how compact country boys affect me. Hell, he's even let me blow him a few times when his wife was out of town.

"How'd the kid end up nekkid, by the way?" Ken rolls down the window. There's a rush of frigid air. He flips out the cigarette, rolls the window back up.

"Clothes came off in the struggle. He was a wildcat."

Ken snickers. "Yeah, right. Sure glad you were able to overpower him."

Jason's head jerks up as I enter the sleeper. "Huhm?" His gagged grunt's got an interrogative sound.

He can't tell it's me. I've taped his eyes so that he won't be able to see any of my buddies or be able to identify them later. Me, well, I was the bait. Seeing me was what caught him. Wouldn't be the first man whose hungers made him vulnerable. So if he lives, if he gets loose, I'm the one who'll fall. Not my boss, not my buds. Me.

"Hey," I say, slipping beneath the covers. "Figured you could do with some cuddling."

I roll us onto our sides, hugging him, soothing him. Shivering, he snuggles back against me, clearly desperate in such terrifying extremity for any sort of kindness. He's probably confused beyond belief, being held and comforted by the very man who pulled a gun on him and abducted him. I finger the moist fur between his buttocks, play with the soft hair on his chest. Beneath my touch, I can feel his heart hammering.

"We're here."

I must have fallen asleep. It's Ken, standing in the doorway of the sleeper. He gives a big grin. "You plugged that boy's butt yet?"

"No." I rub my eyes and rise. "Not yet. I'll be right out."

Ken climbs out of the cab. I hunker down beside my prisoner, running a finger along the bands of tape sealing his eyes
and mouth. "You're going to behave while we work, all right?
If you don't, I'll have to knock you out. We're way out in the
country, so there's no one to hear if you do call for help. If you
give us any trouble, Jason, I'll pistol-whip you, swear to god...
or my buddies will shoot you. The last trucker we got they shot
through the head. You understand? Only way you're going to
survive is do exactly what I say."

Jason gives a pronounced nod. He curls into a fetal position,
takes a deep breath and lies still. I leave him there to help the
guys unload.

It takes a while. Small crew tonight, smaller than usual. By
10:00 p.m., I'm tired, and we're only halfway done. "I've done
my part," I growl, dropping a box and dusting off my hands.
"I'm going to check on the captive."

"Hope you got lube," Ken snickers.

"As a matter of fact, I do."

"Hey, man?" Ken grabs my shoulder. "Are you up to what
needs doing?"

"Not sure. I know it's necessary sometimes. It's just that
he's..."

"Buck, you're so fucking predictable. He's a hot little dude. I
get it. I been waiting for this to happen for years. It was only a
matter of time before you met a mark like him. He's seen you,
man. He ain't seen us. You're the one whose ass is on the line.
Look, the grave's ready. He's got to join the others. You want
me to?"

For just a second it's a welcome proposition, that complete
abdication of responsibility. Ken squeezes my shoulder hard. "I
will, man. If you want. Make it easier on you, y'know?"

"No. If it's got to be done, I'll do it." I shrug off his hand. "See you in a bit."

Jason gives me some fight, but that only arouses me more, encouraging me to be rougher.

"Hold still," I growl, shoving his face into the blanket. We're both naked now, kneeling on the floor of the sleeper. He's bent over the bed's edge. I'm behind him, kneading his buttocks, fingering his fuzzy cleft. He shakes his head, cries out against his gag, writhes beneath me.

"What? You don't want to be fucked? Didn't you beg for this earlier? Do the cuffs and rope and tape make that much difference?" I force him down, slap his ass around, spread his cheeks, bite them, push my tongue up inside his musky, bittersweet butthole. I bite his neck, his shoulders, his back, leaving a wake of teeth-marks and bruises. I work his nipples with one hand, with the other push a lubed finger inside him. I finger-fuck him, slow and deep. Eventually his struggles subside. When I shift a hand to his groin, I find his dick stiff, seeping precum.

I can't help but chuckle. "Starting to like this, huh? Wasn't this what you wanted? Isn't this what you've been aching for all damn night? Haven't you been longing for this ever since you set eyes on me?"

Inside him, I curve my finger, find the little bulge of his prostate, rub it. Jason cocks his ass and gives a deep groan.

"You want me to rape you, don't you, buddy? Beg me to rape you." I pinch a nipple, work a second finger in.

"Mmm!" Nodding frantically, my prisoner bucks back against my probing hand. Another dollop of lube, and we're both greased up. I slide my cockhead up and down his crack, teasing him, nudging his hole. Without warning I shove inside him, faster than I should, making him wince and whimper.

"Hurting? Yeah? *Yeah?* Good. It should hurt a little," I growl, wrapping my arms around his torso, thrusting into him. "*Damn*, you're tight. More? You want more, you little bastard? Want me to fuck you harder?"

Jason's answer is another series of wild nods, another deep groan. Soon I'm pounding his butt so brutally I'm panting like a dog. His ass-muscles clench, gripping and pumping my dick. "Oh, yeah. Sweet boy. Sweet boy!" I groan. "That's *great*. Damn, what a man-milker you are."

The kid's rear-end is as skillful and hungry as his mouth. All too soon, I've shot my load up his butt. I rest atop him for a little bit, taking a breather, before rolling him over and sucking him off.

The crew peels out, Jeeps and pickup trucks rattling over the road's ruts, disappearing over the hill. Ken and I head back inside, survey the piled boxes, flip off the lights. The truck, emptied now, looms beneath the warehouse roof. Inside it, my prisoner waits, his ass no doubt oozing my cum, lying there helpless, wondering about salvation and doom, wondering if the man who just made love to him will return with a gun in his hand.

"Smoke?" Ken says.

"Only if you got a cigar. You know I hate cigarettes."

"You bet. Here you go."

We stand outside, smoking, sharing Ken's ubiquitous flask of rye. The rain's blown over; the sky's cloudless. Winter stars glitter, a cold clarity arcing above us. Our breath turns to fog. We puff on our cigars; their red embers wax and wane.

"Ken?"

"Oh, gawd. I know that tone. No."

"I can't. When you call the boss, tell him—"

"Tell him that you took care of the kid, that he's buried with

the others. Do I know you, or do I know you?" He takes a big
gulp of rye.

"Ken?"

Ken inhales, blows out a great stream of smoke, coughs,
guffaws. "What you gonna do with him? Besides fuck him
cross-eyed?"

"Just did that. Plan to do it again come dawn. I don't know
what I'm going to do. Keep him. Keep him. Keep him captive
till I'm sure he'll stay."

"And if he gets loose, runs off? The end of you, sure as shit.
Once the cops are done with you, the boss'll take his turn. You'll
be the one buried out back."

"Yes, that's true. I'm more than aware of that."

"Piece of tail worth it?"

"This tail, yes." I take a deep breath, let the tobacco fill my
head. "I think so. I'm pretty sure. Yes, I'm sure. He's beautiful. He needs taken care of. He makes me feel...a tenderness I
haven't felt in twenty years."

"A *tenderness*? Oh, hell. Oh, *please*, y'all just met. All right.
Shit. Your funeral. But if anyone finds out, well—"

"I'll say I lied to you. That you didn't know I'd spared him."

Ken nods. We fall silent, passing the flask back and forth
till it's done. A shooting star streaks over. I turn, about to head
back to the truck, when Ken grabs me from behind in a big
bear hug. "Good luck, bud. I'll give you a call next week."
Then he's loping off. His engine starts up, his tires rake gravel
and he's gone.

I flick on the lamp. Jason's not on the bed or beneath the blankets. He's huddled on the sleeper's floor, shaking violently in the
frigid air. Between his stiff nipples, the silver cross twinkles. His
pecs are like little hills, the fur dusting them a forest, a dark fog.

"Tried to get loose, huh?" I stand astraddle him, trying to sound mean. He hesitates, then nods.

"That isn't happening." With some effort, I drag him back onto the bed. "Get back under the covers, or you'll freeze your pretty ass off."

Instead of acquiescing, Jason shakes his head and rubs his taped mouth against my shoulder. He gives a panicked grunt.

"Hold on." I fetch my pocketknife. Carefully, I cut the tape gagging him, peel it off—slowly, so as not to pull his hair and goatee too much—and remove the sodden rag from his mouth.

"Thanks," he gasps. "Oh, man, I really need to piss. And my hands are numb, my wrists are killing me! There's a piss bottle in that there drawer. Please, would you...?"

Poor kid. I unpeel his blindfold. I fetch the bottle, help him stand, hold his limp dick. By the time he's done, he's semierect.

"Could I have some water too? There's some over there."

We sit side by side on the bed. I hold the bottle to Jason's mouth; he gulps and gulps. We share the water till it's gone.

"I'm going to free your hands now. Don't give me any fight, okay?"

"I won't, man. Promise."

Jason groans with relief as I remove the cuffs and loosen the ropes around his arms and torso. He winces as I reposition his arms before him. I rub his chafed wrists and cold hands for a long time.

"Feel better?"

"Yeah, thanks."

"Here," I say, cuffing his hands in front of him, then re-tightening the ropes. "This shouldn't be so uncomfortable. Okay? Better like this?"

Jason nods. I help him stretch out on the bed. Shucking off my clothes, I join him beneath the blankets, wrap him in my arms. We lie still for a while, faces pressed together, body heat building between us. Storm's started up again; sounds like sleet pattering the roof.

"What now?" he says, looking me in the eyes. "Are you gonna shoot me?" After all those frightened tears, now his voice is steady, deep and manly, matter of fact. Such strength in the face of fate makes me want him all the more.

"Depends." I rub my beard across his nose. "You have a choice."

"Tell me."

"I'm expected to shoot you, Jason. We have a hole already dug in the woods, not far from here. You need to know that there were others. They're out there now."

"You killed them?"

"No. But I helped bury them. They gave us trouble. And we couldn't afford witnesses."

"Jesus. Damn," Jason whispers. "So what's the choice? I end up buried in the woods, or what? Can't you just let me go?"

"No. Not yet. Too risky. If you bolt, I'm done for."

"Then what?"

"I...I want to keep you."

"That's the choice?"

"Yes. Captive or corpse."

"Uh, that's a no-brainer. I'd rather you keep me."

"I figured," I say, kissing his brow. "Thing is, your life is in my hands now, but, if I let you loose, *my* life will be in *your* hands. You get that?"

"Sure. So I'd live with you?"

"Yes, though I plan to keep you restrained till I'm sure you won't turn me in."

"So I'd be your hostage? Or your boy? Your lover or your slave?"

I pat his butt, tug his crack-fur. "All those, I think."

Jason snuggles closer. "What about your boss?"

"He'll think I shot you. Before we leave here, I'll fill in that grave in the woods. Maybe later, if things work out between you and me, I'll come clean and let him know the truth. What about the guy you're driving for?"

"Well, I drive for myself. This here truck's mine. But the guy I'm hauling for...I don't know. I guess we can figure that out later. Maybe I'll tell him you knocked me out before I saw your face."

For a few minutes, we're silent. Jason caresses my chest hair; I hug him hard.

"Look, Buck, I've been so, so lonesome," Jason blurts. "Shy guys like me, we don't meet folks easy. This has all been scary as hell...but, *god*, you're hot, and *god*, we're good together...so I'm glad we met, damned glad. I love the way you hold me; I love the way you fuck me. I know a gift when I see it. You frighten me, okay, when I think about some of the things you've done? But, if I'm gonna be your boy, we've gotta trust each other. So, *hell*, keep me cuffed as much as you please. Keep me bound and gagged in your basement, or chained to a post, if it makes you feel safe. Hell, make me your trussed-up cum-dump. Treat me like a captive till you come to trust me. You're sparing my life, so, look, I *owe* you, I'm beholden. I ain't gonna betray you, I swear! I don't want to lose you."

Jason kisses me. I kiss him back, hard. I take his nipples between my fingers. Soon he's gasping, face buried in my chest hair. Suddenly he rolls over, rubs his ass against my groin and whispers, "Please. Please plow me again. Please, Buck? Please? You feel so good inside me. I need you, man. I need your seed up my ass."

* * *

"We'll be home in about two hours. Going to be all right like this?"

Jason gives an affirmative grunt. He's curled on my truck bed, beneath the convenient concealment of the capper, looking warm and snug inside a sleeping bag. I've cuffed his hands behind him again and taped his mouth shut. I've taped his eyes too, just in case, so he won't know where we're going, where we'll end up.

"You'll like my place. It's way back in the woods, near a little pond. Quiet. Private. How about some coffee and sausage biscuits once we get home?"

Jason nods vigorously. "Mmmm *hmm*!"

I close the capper. A light snow's begun, powdering the grass. I look back once, toward the western woods, where my boy might have ended. When I turn, there's the pale sunrise, breaking through cloud. East's the direction we need to go. I climb into the Toyota, slip on dark glasses, cock my baseball cap over my eyes, and drive us out of loneliness, out of doubt, straight into that bright white light.

THE TUGGLE MUGGS MAGIC CAVE RIDE

Jonathan Asche

He was so stunning I barely noticed the giant, fluffy, red monster standing next to him.

I guessed he was a little older than me, early thirties possibly. He was of average height but had an above-average body showcased in blue jeans that conformed to every curve and bulge—namely the curve of his ass and the generous bulge of his crotch. When he smiled his teeth practically glowed, bright white against the backdrop of a black beard. He was smiling now as he walked in little baby steps, his pace set by the little girl in a pink shirt walking between his feet, pulling him toward the person dressed in the monster costume.

And then he looked over and smiled at me.

I smiled back, to be polite, then quickly looked away, embarrassed to have been caught staring. Then I looked back to find him still looking, still smiling—a smile that went right to my cock.

"I wanna go on da Sidewinder, Mommy!" my six-year-old nephew Simon whined.

My sister Sandra shifted her ten-month-old to her other hip.

"Only if your Uncle Evan goes with you," she said, looking at me with an impish smile on her lips. Bitch.

Three more rides and a temper tantrum later we were in the park's food court, located in a village of giant toadstools and two-story Technicolor fiberglass trees. "I think the acid's kicked in," I said.

"What's acid?" my nephew asked.

"Sssshhh!" Sandra hissed, glaring at me. "What do you want to eat?"

I didn't respond immediately. The bearded hunk was once again in my sight, about twenty feet away, leaning against a lamppost that looked like it had been designed by Salvador Dali, licking an ice-cream cone. There was no sign of the little girl he'd been seen with earlier. Somehow, through the crowd of rowdy children, complaining teenagers and harried parents he caught my gaze. A knowing grin spread across his face. He brought his lips to his ice cream, slowly, dragging his tongue over the glistening tower of soft serve, scooping up a dollop of cream and curling his tongue back into his mouth, his eyes never leaving mine. His grin grew into a wide, inviting smile and I thought I could detect a sticky white line of ice cream frosting the edge of his dark mustache. He casually reached for his crotch, nonchalantly adjusting his cock.

My dick swelled.

"Evan, what do you want to eat?" Sandra repeated, annoyed.

That guy's cock, I thought. Out loud I said: "Um, I dunno," and Sandra groaned. My mind was made up when I saw a burger stand housed in the trunk of one of the fiberglass trees, located within spitting distance of the surrealistic lamppost and the bearded hunk leaning against it.

"I'll get a cheeseburger," I said, starting toward the burger tree.

"I want one *too!*" Simon announced, running to catch up with me.

"Sure!" I said, pretending I welcomed his company. This wasn't going to be easy.

My eyes were on the hot bearded man as I waited in line at the burger stand, taking in the contours of his physique, imagining what his body would look like without clothes. He only occasionally looked my way now, but he continued to fellate his ice-cream cone for my benefit. When he sent an innuendo-laden glance my way I nearly came in my pants.

Simon's laughter brought me back to earth. "Uncle Evan your weenie's stickin' up!" he shrieked, pointing at the front of my shorts.

"No it's not," I said curtly, pulling the hem of my T-shirt over my protruding crotch. I didn't need a mirror to know that my face was the color of a pomegranate, just as I didn't need to turn around to know that the girls giggling behind me were doing so at my expense.

A deep, manly voice cut through my shame. "The Tuggle Muggs Magic Cave ride is out of order."

I turned slowly to confront the speaker's gorgeous, bearded face. "Huh?"

"Should be private," he said.

My cock twitched, understanding his meaning.

He started backing away. "Fifteen minutes," he said, tossing the last few bites of his ice-cream cone in a trash can.

I nodded, watching him walk away, mesmerized by his high, round ass, the spell broken when I saw him join up with the little girl in a pink shirt and a petite blonde woman, presumably the little girl's mother, presumably the bearded man's wife.

Married or not, I was meeting him at the Tuggle Muggs Magic Cave.

Five minutes into my lunch I excused myself, claiming I had left my cell phone in my sister's minivan. My sister couldn't let me go that easy, claiming she saw me use my phone earlier and, anyway, why did I need my phone at this particular moment?

"I didn't realize you'd turned into our mother," I said.

Sandra mouthed the words "fuck you" as she handed me the keys to her van.

The Tuggle Muggs Magic Cave was on the other side of the park and it took me over ten minutes to get there. When I didn't see him I panicked, checking my watch as if doing so would make time go backward. I walked around the dormant attraction, which from the outside resembled a warehouse-sized dog turd, telling myself I wasn't *that* late.

The same deep, manly voice I had heard earlier said, "Over here."

He was standing behind an artificial tree at the cave's exit. I let out a sigh of relief though my heart continued to pound full speed, anxiety replaced by excitement.

We said nothing, waiting to make sure no park personnel were nearby before we crept into the cave, easily bypassing the four-foot-high metal blockade erected to keep people out. Music from outside followed us into the cave, the cheery voices of the children's chorus sounding out of place in the deepening darkness. *"Sing wugga mugga hay and you'll have a happy, happy day!"* It might have been funny if we weren't so seriously horny.

When we stopped walking I could barely see him. Even as my eyes adjusted to the dark I could only see a hazy outline—a broad-shouldered, well-built, mouthwatering outline.

I started to introduce myself. "I'm—"

He seized me roughly in his arms and silenced me with a kiss. It was a hard, urgent kiss, the kind of kiss that has a punch of violence. I responded with equal force, plunging my tongue into his mouth, my hands grabbing that firm bubble butt and squeezing. I ground my crotch into his. He was harder than the man-made rock that surrounded us, and so was I.

Cool air hit my skin as my shirt was raised over my chest, his hot mouth biting into one of my engorged nipples the moment it was exposed. I let out a sharp cry, wishing I could immediately suck the sound back into my lungs as I heard it bouncing off the walls. My anonymous playmate warned me to be quiet, but he did so with a smile, his white teeth gleaming in the dark.

I pulled at his shirt, uncovering his ripped torso. "Oh, yes," I sighed, pressing my face between his hard pecs, nuzzling the forest of coarse hair that covered them, inhaling his scent.

He put a hand between my legs, groping my bulging crotch, his rough touch making my cock pulse and my body tremble. His fingers moved lower, below my balls, over my *taint*. He was pressing hard, as if trying to break through the fabric separating his fingers from my asshole. I let out a choked whimper and closed my eyes. Outside the cave a group of children shouted excitedly.

With the quick tug of a button and an even quicker pull of a zipper his hand was inside my pants, rubbing the wet, sticky front of my briefs, and driving me fucking insane. I leaned into him, hunting for another kiss and getting it, hard and deep, the same way I wanted his cock.

My hands went to his pants, so excited to get at the treasure inside I could barely unhook the buttons of his fly. His swollen cock bulged beneath a pair of plaid boxers. Impatiently, I slipped a hand into the fly, gasping when I pulled out his dick. I wished we were someplace brightly lit so I could better see his cock, but even in the darkness I could appreciate its beauty—its length, its thickness, the raised veins on the shaft, the smooth curves of the head. And good as it looked, it felt even better in my hand. I stroked it, rubbing the slick ooze of his precum over the pulsing crown of his cock, loving the sound of him sucking in his breath as the sensation rocketed through him. He was uncut, and I pulled on the collar of foreskin, rolling it over the ridges of his cockhead, eliciting another hiss through his clenched teeth.

A woman's voice forced its way into the cave: "Joshua, if I have to tell you *one more time...*"

I sank to my knees, so eager to suck my mystery man's dick that the discomfort of the ground's rough cement didn't register. His cock was really drooling and I quickly slurped up his salty precum. I flicked the dewy crown and dug into the folds of his foreskin. Then I swallowed him whole.

This time he was the one to cry out, his sudden loud groan reverberating down into the dormant cave. He quickly stifled himself, his moans rumbling in his throat like an idling motorcycle as I took his cock into my hungry mouth. I hooked my hands in his jeans and boxers and tugged, pulling them down past his cock—his hard-on springing upward when it freed itself from the underwear's fly—and leaving them bunched around his knees. His balls were plump and hairy and felt good in my mouth. He let out a squeak of a whimper as I pulled his nut sac tight. His fingers pressed into my scalp. "Easy, now," he whispered.

My hands went to his ass, clasping those globes of muscle and squeezing. His buttcheeks were surprisingly smooth, but the cleft between was lined with fur. I sought out his asshole, poking at the moist pucker, his ass-ring contracting to my touch. He rolled his hips and clenched his butt, holding my fingers in his asscrack, but only briefly. I extricated them long enough to put them in my mouth, hastily returning them, dripping with spit, to his ass and, just as hastily, returning my mouth to his throbbing cock.

I worked a finger into his hole, and he moaned softly. *This is just the prologue*, I thought mischievously. *You'll really have a hard time keeping quiet when I get my tongue up there.*

A child's voice interrupted my filthy musings. "I wanna go in *here!*" she demanded.

"You can't, honey," said her father. "This ride is closed."

My bearded trick whispered, "Stand up." His voice was like distant thunder.

My muscles protested as I got to my feet. Once I was standing he steered me around so that I was facing the cave's bumpy wall. He pulled my shorts down with one quick, decisive jerk. His hands were immediately on my ass, his fingers pushing into the deep divide, rubbing the tight knot of my asshole. I nearly melted into a puddle on the floor.

Then I was biting my lower lip, trying to keep silent as he bore into my ass, face first, plunging his tongue into my hole. A hot, pulsating pleasure seethed through my cock and my balls tingled as he tongue-fucked my hole. Though I was struggling to keep quiet, he ate my ass so ravenously that his wet slurping was practically deafening.

The ass-munching ended as abruptly as it began. And then he was pressing his cock into my ass, rubbing it against my spit-lubricated trench. My butt bobbed against him, massaging his hot pole.

His weight fell across my back. When he spoke his beard tickled my neck. "If I had a rubber I'd fuck you so hard," he breathed into my ear, grinding his cock against my pulsating asshole. "But this feels pretty good."

I couldn't disagree.

He reached around my waist and grabbed my dick, so stiff and swollen it ached. A moan bubbled out of my throat and my knees grew weak. He chuckled softly, pulling on my cock while rubbing his against my ass. His cockhead pushed against my sphincter, my asslips parting slightly, inviting him inside. And I wanted him inside, all the way, pounding my ass, filling my chute with his load. But the teasing pressure of his cock against my asshole felt, as he put it, pretty good too.

His hand on my cock felt amazing. His even, rhythmic strokes reduced me to a big, quivering raw nerve. My dick drooled, my nut sac tightened. I was so close...

But he was closer. His cock dipped into my ass, nudging my sphincter wider, threatening to plunge inside—and I would've happily let him. Then it popped out, sliding up my sweaty asscrack, rubbing up and down between my open buttcheeks, his breathing getting louder and harsher as he humped my ass. Then he had an arm across my chest, pulling me tight against him. He grunted, "Aw, shit," and I felt his warm, creamy load splash down on my ass.

He rested his chin on my shoulder, panting heavily, his cock still pumping out his load. "Oh, yes, oh, yes," he sighed, thrusting his hips against my ass, his dick gliding through his thick, gooey cum oozing between my buttocks.

His chin moved off my shoulder and down my back, his tongue coursing down my spine. And then his face was in my ass again, feeding on spunk, lapping it up loudly. A pig at my trough.

Another snatch of music trickled into the cave. *"Put all your cares away and enjoy our land of fun and play!"*

"Turn around," commanded my trick, steering my body around so that my cock was jutting toward his face. He curled a hand around the shaft and squeezed, smiling as a copious drop of precum leaked out the piss slit. His tongue darted out, snapping up the bead of juice in a quick flick, like a frog catching a fly. After flashing another smile, he opened his mouth and wolfed down my cock.

The pleasure hit me so hard I nearly toppled over. I rested my hands on his shoulders to steady myself, moaning as my dick disappeared down that warm, moist mouth. I thrust my hips forward, my balls hitting his hairy chin, getting closer and closer. My body shuddered, twitching like I'd been electrocuted. My cock erupted.

Moans gurgled deep in his throat as he took my load, swallowing each spurt. He only pulled his mouth away when he was sure he'd drained me dry, but my cock still had more to give, pushing out a final white bead of cum. He snatched that up with his whip-like tongue, licking his lips in the exaggerated fashion of a Vaudeville comic.

When he got to his feet we kissed and I tasted my load on his tongue. My hands went down his back to his ass for another grope, lamenting that I didn't get an opportunity to demonstrate my rimming skills. *Maybe next time*, I thought, hopefully.

He pulled his shirt down over his chest and said: "Guess we better get out of here."

We slipped out of the cave a few minutes later, blinking in the blinding sunlight. A woman with the face of a bulldog and about as much fashion sense saw us and approached. Mistaking us for maintenance employees, she asked if the Tuggle Muggs Magic Cave ride was now operational, and was disappointed to learn that it wasn't. As the woman trudged off, grumbling, my cell phone rang.

"Glad you got your phone," my sister said acidly when I answered. "So where the hell are you?"

"Uh, just got turned around, I guess. I'm over by, um, the Tuggle Muggs Magic Cave."

"Oh, wait there. Simon hasn't been on that ride yet."

"Don't hurry. It's out of order." *But the ride I took worked just fine.*

I hung up the phone and turned to make a comment to my bearded trick, and possibly arrange to hook up again. But he had disappeared, swallowed up by the sea of children, parents and giant fuzzy monsters.

"Sing wugga mugga hay and you'll have a happy, happy day!"

SMALL-TOWN BLUES

Rob Rosen

Got home super late from work, almost morning actually, too worked up to watch TV or read emails. Scanned some Internet porn, but that just made me horny. Worked up and horny: two bad things to be that late at night during the week in a small town, cock out of my boxers, begging for release. Only a solo match seemed a waste of a perfectly good boner. Meaning, I was in my car not a minute later in nothing but a pair of ripped denim shorts and a muscle T-shirt.

It was time to do some cruising.

My options were sadly limited. No gay bars in the sticks. Not even a late-night diner. So I stopped by the park first. There was a bathroom tucked away in a dark corner. Had me some luck there before. You only found horned-up dudes in the park that late at night. Except, this time, the bathroom was empty. I stood outside, cock out, a cool night breeze making it achingly stiff, dripping with sticky spunk.

After twenty minutes with no bites, I headed for a nearby

truck stop. I swaggered past some of the rigs, pushing down on my swollen crotch. I thought I was too late; everyone was tucked away in his cab. Couple of truckers were playing poker by a park bench. Old and fat. *Blech.* Not a good night for being alone and horny.

In other words, I had me the small-town blues. Nix that, make it the small-town blue balls. And mine were full of cum.

"Guess I'll just go home and beat off," I said to myself, dejectedly.

I started my way there, too, but my belly was gurgling. That's when I saw the sign down the street glowing like a beacon: GAS STATION/CONVENIENCE STORE. OPEN 24 HOURS. Salvation. I pulled in, the lot deserted. I walked inside, the bells on the door tinkling, but the place was seemingly empty.

"Hello?" I called out. "Anybody home?"

I heard a noise from down one of the aisles. A shuffling of magazines. A telltale zipper moving either up or down. "Um, be right out," I heard, the voice all croaky, tinged with something foreign. I hightailed it back there, in case there was something worth seeing. What I found was the sole worker, an Indian dude. Not Native American Indian. Indian from India Indian. And boy did he look nervous.

"Stocking the merchandise?" I asked, giving him the once-over. Guy was tall and lean, with hairy forearms, amber skin, dark-green eyes, jet-black hair, tan slacks, red worker's vest. Oh, and a tenting dead center. I looked over at the magazines: a nice array of smut.

"Yes, just stocking. Can I help you find something?" he asked, clearly busted.

I squinted at his name badge. "Uh, maybe a Yoohoo and a cookie, Raj. *Long, hard* day at work." I shot him a wink and a sly smile. He gulped and nodded, leading me around the bend to the items in question. He went back behind the counter. I returned to the magazines, retrieving an issue of *Hung Dudes* that I smacked down on the counter, my chocolaty drink and equally chocolaty cookie right next to it. Again he gulped, then rung me up.

I paid. He handed me the change, his fingers brushing mine, a volt of adrenaline riding shotgun down my back. "Must suck working this late, huh?" I asked.

He sighed. "Very boring, sir. Almost no customers this late."

"Gets lonely, huh?" I practically purred. "Thank goodness for the magazines, right?" I pointed to mine, flipping open one of the pages. Hunter smiled up at us, steely cock in his grip, his finger up his chute. I glanced over at Raj, locking eyes with him, my own cock now just as steely as Hunter's.

"Please do not tell on me, sir," he squeaked out, knowing full well that the jig was up. "I need this job. I need the money."

I shrugged. "You scratch my back, I'll scratch yours."

He looked at me, confused. "I do not know that expression. Sorry."

I leaned across the counter, my hand cupping his crotch. He jumped and nearly fell over. "I think you know what I mean, Raj," I said, watching as he regained his balance.

He nodded, big Adam's apple rising and lowering in his throat. "You will not tell if I do something for you, yes?"

"For me, to me. Something like that," I replied. "Is there a bathroom in this place?"

He shook his head. "For employees only." He pointed to the camera above his head. "I cannot let you use ours, sir, and I cannot use the one outside."

I sighed. "What time do you get off, Raj?"

"Five o'clock, sir. In just under an hour." He nodded, a nervous smile plastered across his handsome, thin face; teeth shockingly white against all that lovely light brown.

"Meet me at the park then, Raj," I told him. "Okay? There's a bathroom at the far west corner." I turned around, my own smile radiant. "That camera doesn't see down that aisle I found you on, does it?"

"No," he managed. "No, sir, it doesn't."

I turned and headed that way. I waited. Nothing. "Down here, Raj," I yelled. He was there a second later, eyes wide with anticipation. "Stand over here, Raj, with your hands on the magazine rack, okay?"

Again he nodded, doing as I said, fingers fairly trembling as he held on, slightly leaning in. I moved behind him, my hands reaching around to his front. His legs were bouncing as I unhooked his belt and zipped down his zipper. The baggy slacks fell to the ground, his button-down shirt lifted up, revealing white briefs, dark legs, way hairy, rife with lean muscle and sinew. "What if someone comes in, sir?" he whispered, voice shaky, lilting in that beautiful Indian way of his.

"At four in the morning, Raj? Unlikely." I crouched down behind him. "Hold your shirt up for me, Raj," I told him. He held on to the magazine shelf with one hand, his shirt with the other. I cupped his tiny ass with my hands, gave him a spank, then pulled down the material, dropping it to his bunched up slacks. I stroked his ass that was covered in a soft, brown down. He moaned, spreading his legs apart as much as possible, jutting his ass out for me.

"Please, sir. I will meet you at the park just after five. We cannot do this here. It is too dangerous," he nearly cried, head turned back, eyes drilling down into me.

"Show me your asshole, Raj," I told him.

"At five, sir, please."

"Now *and* at five, Raj," I said, willing my voice to stay even.

He released his shirt and the magazine shelf, then reached behind and pulled apart his cheeks for me. His asshole winked out from within, dark pink, haloed with hair. I stood up and inched in, my fingers massaging his hole, my other hand reaching around to stroke his cock. The thing was thin and monstrously long. He groaned upon contact. "See you soon, Raj," I whispered in his ear, then turned and walked out, the doorbell tinkling yet again.

I sat in my car and watched the store. Raj returned to his counter. He smiled nervously at me and waved. I pointed at my watch, then drove off, exhaling at last. I sniffed my fingers as I made my way down the road. Raj's ass lingered, sweet and delectable. A foreign smell. Different. In a small town like mine, something to covet. I smiled as I sucked on my digits, reaching the park a short while later.

Only mine wasn't the only car there.

I parked and got out. It was still dark outside, the only light coming from a small bulb outside the bathroom. My heart thumped madly inside my chest, my fingers twitching inside the pockets of my shorts. I scanned the park as best I could, but it was silent and empty, black as coal. *Must be in the bathroom,* I said to myself.

I made some noise so he'd know he wasn't alone. Then I went in. Dude was up against the urinal. Only, I couldn't hear any pee. No shocker there. I mean, just past four in the middle of a park; it could really only mean one thing. "Howdy," I said, my voice echoing around the barren concrete room.

He jumped in place. "Howdy," he replied, voice trembling.

I gave him the once-over. Short guy, barely five feet tall. Thin as a twig. A touch of gray in his hair. Thank goodness. Not my type. Not by a mile. Damn. Like going to an ice-cream shop and all they have is vanilla. And I hate vanilla. But I did have to pee, so I went to the stall next to him, looking over and down. Guy was hard as granite too, and packing, his cock like a fifth limb jutting out of his tiny frame.

"Big things, little packages," he said, turning to look at me. He was cute, in an elfin way. Probably early forties, glasses, wedding ring, eyes a vivid blue, like the ocean in Tahiti. The kind of blue you want to take a dip into. "Wanna taste?" he asked.

I finished peeing and shook my head. "Um, I have a date already."

He looked about the bathroom. "You sure about that? Seems to be just you and me out here."

"I'm early. He'll be here soon enough." I backed away, washed my hands and looked over at him. "Sorry, big guy."

He frowned and shoved his whopper back inside his jeans. "But we have time now, right. Just let me blow you." Man, and I thought I was horny as fuck. "I'll, um, I'll pay you even."

Now that I had to laugh at. Still, it did give me an idea. "How much?"

He reached for his wallet. "Fifty?" But the wallet was a good deal thicker than that.

"Tell you what. Make it two hundred and I promise you one hell of a show." I walked outside. He followed close behind. I ambled to a nearby picnic table and grabbed on to the far side. "Lift the other end and follow me," I told him. He put his wallet away and did as I said, both of us setting the table down a short distance from the bathroom, another dim bulb lighting the area for about ten feet around, then nothing but trees and a lone cricket or two.

He walked back over to me and looked up. "Two hundred for a show? What kind of show?"

I smiled, bent down, and brushed my lips against his. "You'll see, big guy," I told him. "You'll see." I looked around, but knew we were alone. And if someone else should show up, they'd be looking for the same thing we were. Not even the cops were up at this time of night. Small-town blues even reached them. "On the table, big guy. Best seat in the house."

He swallowed, turned and sat on top, eyeing me the whole time. Dude looked like a scared little rabbit. A scared, little rabbit with a horse-hung dick, but still. Fuck, he even made Raj look tough. "Now what?" he asked, voice barely above a whisper, eyes darting.

"Now you get naked, big guy. And we wait for the show."

He stood and started to leave. "I, um, I need to get home. Maybe next time. This, uh, this wasn't such a good idea after all."

I moved in and grabbed his shoulders, bending down to lay a heavy-duty kiss on him, mouths thrashing, tongues colliding. He melted into me, his body relaxing. I moved back half an inch. "Now get naked for me, okay?" I said into his ear, biting down on a tender lobe. "I promise, you'll enjoy this."

He paused, but did as I asked, moving in reverse, staring at me all the while. He kicked off his sneakers first, then reached for his T-shirt, lifting it above his head. His torso was pale like the moon, hairless save for a smattering dead center, nipples pink and thick, muscles squat and tight. His jeans popped open next, then slid down and off, his boxers tenting something fierce. Then those, too, were kicked off, as were his socks. He had runner's legs, hairless, thin; small feet; bony knees; and cock for days.

"Where do you get enough blood to fill that thing?" I asked.

He gave it a stroke. "I can suck it, too. Wanna see?"

I stared up at the sky and gave a silent thanks. The night was proving very interesting indeed. "A pre-show," I quipped. "Goody."

He sat on the bench, one foot on the seat, the other he started to lift up to place behind his neck, yoga-like. Hunched over now, he had little distance to go to get his mouth to that giant cock of his. I watched in stunned awe as he took it in and gave it a suck, the sound of slurping filling the night air around us. It was then that I heard another car pulling up. "Stay just like that," I whispered. He froze, but did as I said, cockhead still inside his mouth.

Then I waited, heart pumping loudly in my ears, prick straining inside my shorts. I breathed a sigh of relief when Raj turned the corner. He jumped and froze. "I, uh, I made it. Just as promised, sir." He looked at me, eyes wide. "Who is this? And, um, how is he doing *that*?"

Mister monster cock popped his out of his mouth. "Lester," he replied. "And it takes some practice."

"And a big dick," I added.

"I can see that," said Raj, unsure of what to do next. "But maybe I should just go home, yes? Maybe we can meet later, sir, okay?"

"No," I said.

"No," Lester echoed, again sucking his dick as he watched the two of us.

"This is not good, sir," Raj said. "Even less safe than store. Please, later, okay?"

I moved in and put my arms around him, our faces up close now; he was breathing heavy, body fairly trembling. "It's okay, Raj," I said, the most tender kiss placed on his lips. He froze, but then relented, swapping some heavy spit soon enough. "Now go stand with your back against the wall, okay? Just beneath the lightbulb, so me and Lester can get a good look at you."

He hesitated, but walked over, back against the cement, hands at his sides. I stared at him. He stared back. "Will you be fucking me, sir?" he yelled out. "I brought some rubbers from the store."

I looked over at Lester. He nodded, his mouth going deep down on his prick. Then I looked back over at Raj. "Get naked for me, Raj. Leave the rubber on the ground to your side." Again he hesitated, but horniness ruled out. As it always did. Case in point: little guy Lester scrunched up naked on a park bench, cock in mouth.

Raj slipped off his red vest and laid it on the ground. Then he reached inside his slacks, took out the rubber and set it down, too. He unbuttoned his shirt next, revealing a slim chest and slim belly, furry, dense with compact muscles, everything honey colored, deep and rich. The shirt joined the vest just before he kicked off his shoes and slid out of his slacks, then his briefs. Again he stood there, arms at his sides, naked save for his black socks, boner jutting up and out, arcing to the side, easily nine inches, brown balls hanging low.

I moaned at the sight of him. As did Lester from behind me. Then both of them watched as I got undressed, until there were three naked strangers cruising each other outside a park bathroom in the middle of fucking nowhere, all with raging hard-ons, one firmly entrenched up its owner's mouth. You couldn't help but laugh. And moan, yet again.

I moved in, my hands reaching for Raj's. I lifted them up and held them above his head. "Keep them there, Raj," I whispered, mouth to mouth, eye to eye.

"Okay, sir. I will keep them here," he whispered, pressing his lips into mine, body quaking as I moved my hands from his and yanked hard on his big, brown nipples. Then I backed up an inch, taking his body in. Truly, he was stunning to behold, rich and exotic, fur laden, and hung like an ox. My hands roamed it all, running through his soft matting, fingers tracing each tiny muscle in turn, causing him to both giggle and groan simultaneously.

Then I crouched down and sucked on his nearly purple knob, salty precome hitting the back of my throat like a bullet, working the length of his cock in and down as far as I could, a happy gagging tear streaming down my cheek. His moan swirled around my head. As did Lester's, dimmer in the distance. "Please fuck me, sir," Raj pled.

I yanked on his swaying nuts, popping his prick out of my mouth. "Damn, everyone's so fucking horny around here tonight," I said, with a grin, licking his piss slit. "Small-town blues," I added, reaching for Raj's sides and then turning him around. Then he placed his palms against the concrete, legs wide, ass out. So fucking beautiful. I kissed his hole, sucked it, licked it, tongue-fucked it until it was good and wet, and then reached for the rubber. "Ready, Raj?"

His body trembled, ass jiggling. "Yes, sir."

"Ready, Lester?" I yelled over my shoulder.

I heard him pop his dick out of his mouth. "Fuck, yeah," the little guy shouted, then went back to sucking.

I stood up and leaned my body into Raj's, my white against his brown. I spat into my hand and lubed my sheathed prick up. Then I placed the tip against his asshole. I reached around and tugged at Raj's nipples as I entered him, soft and gentle, just the head. He sucked in his breath and tightened his ring around me, causing every nerve ending in my body to shoot off like the Fourth of July. Then he relaxed and I slid it all the way home, tweaking his nips. "Feel good, Raj?" I whispered in his ear.

"Oh, yes, sir. That feels so good," he lilted, reaching down now to stroke his giant billy club of a dick. "Come inside me, sir. Please."

I hummed, my cheek against his back, sliding my cock in and out, in and out. "No problem, Raj. No problem at all."

Then I let him have it with both guns, ramming and cram-ming my cock inside of him, each thrust eliciting a gasp from him, a moan from me, a groan from Lester, the park alive with our sexual symphony. He picked up the pace on his cock while I piston-fucked him and tortured his nipples. Soon enough, his knees started to buckle, his body slick with sweat.

"I am going to come now, sir," he growled, back spasming, the sound of his come splattering the wall, *splat, splat, splat.* His hole gripped my cock like a vise, jacking it until I filled that rubber with every last ounce of come I had in my balls, howling as I came, ramming deep, deep inside of him, both of us panting, trying to catch our breaths. Then I eased out of him and turned him around, mashing my mouth into his.

A minute passed by, then two. I pulled away. "Better now, Raj?" I cooed.

He smiled, stroking my lower back. "Much better, sir."

I turned. Poor Lester was still going at it. "Need some help, Lester?" I yelled over to him.

He nodded, still sucking as we walked on over. I stood on one side, Raj on the other. I spit in my hand, lubed up Lester's exposed little hole, and slid my index finger inside. Raj yanked on his nuts and jacked his shaft, the part that wasn't buried inside Lester's mouth. It didn't take long them. Lester moaned, deeply, compact body quaking, eyes fluttering as he came, gobs of jizz oozing from between his lips before gliding down his chin. Then he extricated himself from his precarious position and collapsed backward onto the table, panting, giant cock thrusting straight up. Seriously, it was enough to take your very breath away.

Still, business was business.

I turned and retrieved Lester's wallet. "Some show, huh, Lester?" I asked.

"Make it three hundred," he yelled, still prone, cock finally drooping.

I chuckled and emptied his wallet, walking back over to Raj, who was watching me intently, still naked, still semihard, amazingly. "I think you need this more than I do," I said, now stroking his hefty tool.

He took it, his face lighting up, the sky at last turning from black to heavy blue. "Yes, sir. I do indeed, sir," he replied, his striking voice like music to my ears. Then he kissed me, deep and hard, my soft schlong held tight in his grip. "And maybe I can learn that nice little trick from Mister Lester," he added, green eyes searching, eager. "For next time."

Lester at last sat up, smiling, gooey spunk still dripping from his chin. "Take's a lot of practice, Raj," he said.

Raj laughed, as did I. I pulled him into me, good and tight. "Not like there's much else to do in this tiny town, Lester," I said. "Is there, Raj?"

"No, sir," came the reply. "All the time in the world, sir."

"And one huge dick to work with," I couldn't help but add.

"And that too, sir," he agreed. "And certainly that."

BULLY

Mark Wildyr

Like always after last-period math, I had to hide my condition with my books. The solid, athletic form of Rex Lundgren sitting one row ahead of me and one seat to the right sent my brain into orbit, made my mouth drool and started my cock beating a steady tattoo against my pants. Handsome, the Vikings' star quarterback and the sexiest hunk on the Palo Verde College campus—that was Rex. Those qualities ought to be fairly apportioned out to three different men, not invested in one stuck-up bully.

What made today different from all the others was that when I headed for my car in the parking lot, I ran right into the good-looking fucker as he trotted out from between two cars. His fault, not mine. But that didn't matter.

"Watch where you're going! Queer," he added when he saw who he'd bumped into.

"Takes one," I snapped. Crap, did I really say that out loud? There wasn't anything remotely queer about this Nordic phallic symbol.

I'd gone through high school and college with this guy without exchanging two words. Now I had his full attention. "What'd you say?" The parking lot, so busy moments before, was now a vast, deserted expanse.

"Nothing." I scrambled to pick up the books and the Cross pen I'd lost in the collision. A couple of pages of class notes fluttered away in the breeze like so much trash.

"You called me a queer, you fucker." A scowl made his face mean—but it was a handsome mean.

"Look—" I straightened up, trying to control the shakes caused by such close proximity to almighty Thor...or maybe it was simply terror at Rex Lundgren's towering anger.

"No, *you* look, you pissant pansy. Nobody calls me a queer." He punctuated his words with a hard finger to my sternum, driving me back against the side of my car. The heretofore bright, promising day clouded over.

"Why are you coming down on me, man?" I wheezed. "It was an accident. You like bullying people or something?" *Run for your life, Toby Long*, every fiber of my body screamed. My feet, however, were struck dumb.

"In case you didn't know, asshole, I hate queers. You like rubbing up against me or something?"

That struck too close to the truth. "Not as much as you, apparently."

Suddenly I was lying on the tarmac amid trash and tires and the underbellies of automobiles. It took a minute to realize he'd slugged me. My jaw began to ache; oily pebbles dug into my back. Rex loomed over me, arms on his hips, hard blue eyes signaling outrage.

I started the awkward process of laboring to my feet, weak with relief when Rex turned and strode toward the football field in long, graceful strides. Ignoring the pucker of shame across my shoulders, I once again retrieved my property.

Why was I labeled a homosexual when the only guy I'd ever done anything with was Rod Brigham, a neighbor kid two years ahead of me in school who was so jealous of his precious macho image he wouldn't have breathed a word to anybody? I could still taste his cum on my lips even though he'd moved away last fall.

I got in my '99 Corolla and headed for the apartment I'd talked my folks into letting me rent, even though we lived just across town. I'd wanted to be on my own for my senior year. The apartment was usually a comfortable nest. But after I got my homework done, I was restless. I sat chewing on a piece of bread loaded with peanut butter and jelly and wishing I could smear it all over my cock and lick it off. Unfortunately, I'm not that limber.

Before the sun was completely down, I knew I couldn't stay at home alone tonight. I was too pumped by my exchange with Rex for that. So I gave in to a fantasy I'd been nursing ever since I'd discovered the glory hole john at the Palacio Hotel. I'd never really checked it out, and tonight would be a good time.

The El Palacio had once been the queen of Albuquerque hotels. Now, it was merely seedy—elegant seedy, mind you— but seedy nonetheless. I found a parking place a block away and made like I was headed for the movie complex on Central and First SW but darted into the hotel lobby instead. I was convinced a thousand eyes watched me as I tripped down the stairs to the basement men's room like I really needed to go.

Large, cracked white and black tiles, some yellowing with age, checkerboarded the floor. Three stalls lined the south wall, the last two connected by that intriguing hole. The sinks were directly opposite, so you could get a glimpse of anyone washing his hands and staring back at you in the mirrors. The urinals were out of sight on the west wall.

The place was deserted tonight, and I was half relieved. I wasn't very good at that cruising shit. I took the last booth and pulled down my trousers, but I didn't sit down on the stool. Already half hard, I stuck it through the hole and imagined someone on the other side was about to wrap his tongue around it. I almost hurt myself jerking it out and plopping down on the commode when the door opened.

How in the hell would I hide my bone if the guy came into the other stall? He did, and there wasn't much I could do except to lean forward and hide my condition with my arms. That also gave me a pretty good peek into the other side.

The guy stood and took out his cock like he was going to piss. Then he shook it a couple of times, and it started growing. He slipped his trousers down and stood playing with himself. My prick was standing at attention again. All I could see of the guy were good thighs, a whopper of a cut dick, a couple of fuzzy balls and a flat stomach with a real six-pack. His bush was a light-brown color. Bombshell! I didn't know what his face looked like, but what I *could* see was prime beef.

He didn't fuck around; he walked up to the glory hole and stuck the tip of his big cock through. It was bulbous with a big slit. I swallowed hard and leaned over to run my tongue over it. That was all he needed; he shoved the rest of it through the hole, and I'll swear there were over six inches of cock on my side of the stall, and the wall must have been half an inch thick. This stud was hung.

I took his cock in my mouth and then rode down the long, fat pole until there wasn't any more to take. Then I came back to the end and looked at the thing. It was almost as straight as a ruler, but had a little upward tilt at the end. A brown mole decorated the flat top about halfway down the length of it.

He gave a hunch or two against the other side of the stall, so I quit examining him and began sucking. The dude got so excited he began fucking my mouth. I thought he was going to come through the wall. He must have worked for ten minutes before I heard some muffled noises and his hot, white cum shot out into my mouth. I thought I wasn't going to be able to take it all, but I managed. When he went still, I pulled off of him to take another look at that big cock. As I watched, another dollop of cum oozed out of the end, so I licked it off. Then he pulled out and bent over to get his pants, I tried to get a look at his face, but he was too quick. Oh, well, I'd get a peek when he washed up. But he banged out of the stall and left the men's room without pausing at the basins.

Desperate for a look at him, I jerked my pants back in place and exited the restroom, passing a trim, dark man in his late twenties as I went. I felt his eyes on me as I ran up the stairs, but I needed to see the hunky dude I'd just blown. Too slow. He was gone. Suddenly aware my erection was showing through my pants, I went to my car and jerked off. Fortunately, the old Corolla's windows were smoked to the max.

Friday afternoon, I boarded a bus with a load of Palo Verde students bound for an out-of-town football game with our archrival, the San Luis College Bulldogs. The most enduring memory of the trip was Rex "The Viking" Lundgren's fantastic, broken-field touchdown run in the fourth quarter to give us the game. Man, he was something. Even the padding and the helmet couldn't obscure his physical beauty.

On the seventy-five-mile trip back home that night, victory chants and wild-eyed excitement eventually gave way to quiet conversations, necking and an occasional snore. Regretfully, the athletes were in the bus in front of us; Rex's presence would have been exciting even if he did look down his nose at me.

Half asleep, I got an instant erection when a knee touched my leg. Rory Mason, my seatmate, was zonked, and on the last curve his leg rode up against mine. My entire body quivered like a strummed guitar.

I peered at Rory through the gloom: Mousy hair, slim. Nothing to get excited about...except that I was. Crap! He was kind of cute. Smooth, sallow skin. No pimples for this kid. Tennis player. Decent chest. My cock got harder and my legs involuntarily scissored, pushing against him. He mumbled and halfway turned in his seat. Now his hip rode against me.

When we arrived at the Palo Verde parking lot. Rory accepted my offer of a ride since he lived a couple of blocks from me, but I chickened out and didn't approach him. Hell, I didn't know how.

All hotted up from two sets of stimuli—the recollection of Sexy Rex romping over the goal line and Mousy Rory's leg riding up against me—I didn't go to the apartment. Despite the late hour, I headed straight for the Palacio. I didn't know if the men's room was locked up this time of night, but I was going to find out.

It was open, but deserted. I took a seat, hoping somebody hot and hunky would show up. I sat there playing with myself... getting hard and then letting it go soft before pumping it back up again...for half an hour. I was about to give it up when the door opened and someone came inside. I didn't dare put my eye to the glory hole, but I scrunched down so I could see as much as I could of the dude who entered the stall next to mine. Denims. Muscle shirt. Promising.

Then I got downright excited when he stood facing me and shoved his pants down. Even looking through a hole in dim light, I recognized that cock. It had a brown mole on it, and I was willing to bet it had a little crook near the end when it got hard.

The guy rubbed his hands over his thighs, played with his light-brown bush, lifted his heavy balls and let his cock get stiff. Then he walked right into that hole and tried to fuck my face through half an inch of plywood. What he couldn't manage for himself, I did for him. I sucked his cock like it was a strawberry Popsicle, and I wanted to take it all before it melted.

He was more vocal this time. I heard him groaning and moaning. I even think I heard him cussing a little, but I didn't care. I just wanted to take him over the edge. And just like last time, he came like a gusher. I slurped like crazy, but still, some of him seeped out of the corners of my mouth. This time, he didn't just jerk his cock out of the hole. He remained pressed against the wall while I licked and sucked him until he was half soft. Then he backed up and seemed to hesitate. Was that an invitation?

I jumped up and stuck my leaking cock through the hole, expecting to feel a warm mouth or at least a warm fist. But I just stood there pulsing in the air. I didn't even know he'd left until I heard the outside door slam. I wanted to catch him; maybe see him and say something to him, but I was torn between that wish and my prick's demand. My cock won. I jerked off with three vivid images in my mind's eye: Rex's uniformed butt as he scampered across the goal line, cute Rory's smooth cheeks, and that throbbing cock I'd sucked so good that the guy just stood there leaning helplessly against the stall until he recovered. I shot all over everything in the best orgasm ever. After that, I stumbled up the stairs and went home.

Monday morning when I parked on campus, the impossible happened. I clipped the Viking with my door when I got out of the car. Like a fucking fool, I scrambled over to him, concerned

I'd hurt him. Big mistake. Big, *big* mistake!

"You motherfucking queer shit! You did that on purpose."

"Sorry, Rex, I didn't." I touched the arm he was massaging. Even bigger mistake. A whopper.

He shoved me away. "Don't touch me with those faggot fingers."

"Look, Rex, it was an accident, and I apologized. What more do you want from me?" Suddenly, I had the urge to offer to suck his cock. But that would likely go *way* past whopper.

"Not a fucking thing," the Viking said calmly.

I saw this one coming and got my head partially out of the way so he rattled my cage but didn't put me down. Instinctively, I lashed out; and my knuckles ground against teeth. Man, I'd have been better off offering to blow him. My heart plummeted into my belly and my balls tried to climb up inside me.

The rage in Rex's incredibly blue eyes faded into a look of grim satisfaction. He got me in the heart, belly, and the heart again...one, two, three. I swayed like a battered old punching bag until he got tired of hitting me. When he quit, I ended up on my knees.

Aware I was suddenly alone, I started crawling to my feet, flinching violently when a hand grasped my arm. The wildness left my eyes as Rory Mason helped me up.

"You okay?" he asked, leaning me against my car fender and stooping to pick up my books. "Man, I couldn't believe you stood up to Rex Lundgren."

"Can't exactly say that," I mumbled, examining my jaw with a palm. It seemed to work okay; all my teeth were in their proper place.

"You got him at least once. Split his lip."

"Shit!" That would probably earn me a beating every day for the rest of the year. Great, Long!

Of course, what happened was all over school before the next class bell rang. Giving the Viking a fat lip might not have been the smartest thing I'd ever done, but it made me a hero to Rory. That was okay; he was a likeable guy and really kind of handsome in an understated way. It was flattering. I'd never had a friend who looked up to me like that.

Rex didn't lay any more beatings on me, but he humiliated me at every opportunity, muscling me aside in the hallway and scaring me shitless in the men's room.

"Why?" I asked him one day. "What did I ever do to you?"

"Fags turn my stomach."

"What makes you think I'm queer? I never came on to you or anything."

"Give it up. I *know*, Long. I know. But if you want to put this behind us, meet me in the field house at eleven Friday night."

Palo Verde is a small school with a football field to match. I prefer the grass at field side instead of the bleachers, and Rory joined me there for Friday night's game. In the fourth quarter, the game got tight. As usual, that's when Rex put it in gear. He romped, he threw, he kicked, he played his ass off. I got hard watching him, and Rory noticed. He stared at my crotch a moment before he flushed and looked away. Luckily, Rex broke free and in the pandemonium that followed, things more or less returned to normal.

By game's end my head was so filled with images of Rex, I knew I had to go meet him at the field house, even if it was another mistake. When it was coming up on eleven, I ditched Rory, practically shoving him out of the car. He looked at me through hurt, brown eyes, but I didn't care. Getting to the field house had suddenly become very important to me.

I parked behind the low, cinderblock building on the west side of the football field that housed the football team's locker and equipment rooms. The place looked deserted, but Rex's red Le Baron sat silent and foreboding to my right. The dark, deserted football field appeared ominous somehow. The silent expanse of rich grass gave the night an olive hue. I peered through the single windowpane in the door. There was a light in the back. Uncertain of what awaited, I entered. The door closed behind me with a thunk.

Rex appeared at the doorway of the shower room still drying his hair with a towel. Another scrap of terrycloth circled his waist. "Oh, it's you. Lock the fucking door."

Certain I was sealing my own doom, I did so and then trailed after him. He paused in the dressing area, and his mouth turned down in a sneering smile when he saw me take in his light-brown eyes, broad chest and chocolate nipples. My entire body tensed with fear and anticipation.

"I say you're a queer," he said after a long moment. "You claim you're not. Now I'm gonna prove it."

Rex pulled the towel free, and my eyes went straight to his heavy, circumcised cock. His balls were so big that his penis hung at a forty-five-degree angle while totally flaccid. The hair on his chest narrowed to nothing at his deep navel and picked up again below it to flow into a pale-brown curly bush. Strong, solid thighs; shit, *everything* was strong: flat belly, tapered legs, narrow waist, flaring rib cage. They all exuded power. His big cock had a brown mole on top. Overjoyed, I started grinning.

My joy died when he snarled, "Go on, take it."

"Hell, Rex, you don't have to—"

He put a hand on the top of my head, forcing me to my knees. A little snarky at the way he was acting, I nevertheless lifted his fat cock and licked the bottom of his cockhead.

"Shit, man, get to it! Do what a fairy does." He cupped his

hands at the back of my head and pulled me into him. His cock disappeared into my mouth. "That's more like it," he grumbled, beginning to stiffen.

When his big cock stood out like a branch on a tree trunk, I lost my resentment and let myself go. He must have liked the way I sucked his cock at the Palacio. Now, I'd really give him a ride. I sucked his balls, licked his belly, tweaked his nipples, and stroked his firm pecs. Then he took over, ordering me to knead his balls and play with his ass while he held my head in both hands and fucked my face, releasing all of his pent-up violence. Rex was getting head and punishing queers and exploring unsuspected passions all with the same fucking. He rammed me hard and deep, almost bruising my throat. But when he came, I forgave him. In the oddly vulnerable moments when his cum was shooting through his rock-hard cock, he groaned and clasped me tight against him, and some small dollop of human feeling leaked out with his semen. We were friends, companions, lovers.

"You've been on cloud nine since I told you to meet me, haven't you?" He pulled away and started stroking himself again. "Take your clothes off."

He wanted to see me naked. Maybe he'd watch while I beat if off. I shivered as I stripped.

Rex walked right into me. His semi-hard cock kissed my instant erection. Our bellies touched. Then he tripped me, and I fell backward onto a thick mat smelling of sweat and masculine bodies. He landed on top of me. His chest on mine excited me something crazy. Slowly, he dragged his body up mine, his cock stroking my groin, my navel, my sternum, my neck before he presented himself. I opened my jaws and accepted his veined, swollen monster. Immediately, he rammed himself down my throat. He hesitated a moment and then withdrew to the very tip. I swabbed his cock with my tongue and felt him quiver. I pulled him back into me. He set up a rhythm as I played with his full, firm balls and hard buttocks.

Suddenly, he came up and off me. Sitting on my groin, he rubbed his big cock over my belly and chest. "Turn over," he ordered roughly, rising to his knees. "I wanna see your girly butt."

If he hadn't put it that way, I might have willingly obeyed, but there was nothing feminine about my butt. He saw the rebellion and reacted. A palm stung my cheek. His class ring set my jaw to aching.

"Turn over, you fucking asshole."

He moved between my legs as I obeyed. I relaxed as his strong hands played over my back, moving lower to cup my buns.

"Smooth like a baby," he laughed, parting my cheeks. Suddenly, he leaned forward to insert his cock into the fold. I yelped. He slapped the back of my head before pulling my cheeks apart. The bulbous head of his prick at my crack made it quiver like a tuning fork. Without warning, he lunged, setting me aflame. I reared up on my hands; he pressed his chest to my back. Even in the midst of the searing pain, I was conscious of his nipples, the heavy pecs. He lunged again.

"I'm in," he said, his lips tickling my earlobe. As he paused, I relaxed a little, and the pain faded, although it felt as if my insides were filled to the bursting point. "You got my cock in you. How's it feel? You like it? This was your sick, faggot fantasy, wasn't it?"

"Uhhh!" was all I managed. I fell back to the mat, resting my cheek on my forearm. His tongue invaded my ear.

"You like that, queer? Well, you haven't seen anything yet. You're about to be fucked by a man."

Rex Lundgren, Viking, quarterback and school stud began

proving his boast. He pulled out of me and then slowly buried his cock all the way to the balls. His stones spanked me; his bush scratched my buns. I grew acutely aware of everything that was happening: his strong thighs rubbing the inside of my legs, his hard belly mashing my ass, his chest hair tickling my back, his breath in my ear. This handsome, hunky man might sneer and bluster and curse me, but it was *me* he was fucking, me who'd sucked that beautiful cock. He gave up his girls to bury his hard, hot cock in me. It was me he was panting over, me who was bringing him to a climax. He...was...with...me! I began to meet him as he thrust. I fucked the mat, accepting him; enjoying him, glorying in his attention.

"Tell me you like it."

"I...I like it, Rex! I like it!"

"Like what, queer?"

"Like your big cock! Like you fucking me."

"So act like it."

I did. I bucked wildly, meeting each stroke, riding the mat, sensitizing my nerves. "Oh, shit!" I moaned, just before I lost it. "Fuck!"

"What?" he demanded. And then my internal muscles stroked his cock like an invisible hand. He shouted obscenities as his sperm shot into my channel. We bucked and rolled and groaned through our respective orgasms. Nothing had prepared me for the length, the intensity, the brilliance of such an ejaculation. Stars burst on the back of my lids, electricity crackled through me. At long last, it died away.

Rex lay with his full weight atop me. He panted, his breath warm and moist in my ear. It had been wonderful...for *him*, too. Now he'd have to stop treating me like pond scum. I could feel his heart beating with my own, slowly settling back to normal. I ground my butt against him sensuously.

When he spoke, his voice was almost normal. "Brigham said you sucked but wouldn't fuck. I bet him twenty I could prove him wrong. Made you like it, too." With that, he stood. "Clean up the mat and get outta here before I come out of the shower. You don't, I'm gonna kick your ass all over the field house."

"But Rex, you like what we did. I *know* it. I'm the guy you were cruising down at the Palacio. I sucked you there...twice. And now, tonight—"

"You fucking liar!" he roared. "You keep your faggot mouth shut. Hear?" He landed a blow to my naked stomach, and I went down fighting for air. He hauled me up by the hair of my head and shoved me toward the door. "You get outta here, queer. And I hear any of those lies around here, I'll fucking kill you." The rage in those blue eyes terrified me before he stomped off toward the showers.

I was so lethargic I barely managed to get dressed before his shower went off. I beat a hasty retreat to my car where I gathered my shaken, disillusioned ego and drove home. Most of the night I spent reliving the ecstasy and the agony of the evening. Rod Brigham had betrayed me. Instead of Rex's desire for me being real, it was some sick bet between the two of them. Rex fucked me to prove he could. Did they talk on the phone, or did they write? Was my dogged devotion to Rod Brigham set down in letters somewhere?

Then I frowned into the darkness. Then why had he come to get his cock sucked through a glory hole at the Palacio? That meant something, didn't it? Maybe he was just embarrassed. Tomorrow, he'd probably apologize and let me suck him again. Or even fuck me.

Quit kidding yourself, Long. Rex Lundgren might have enjoyed fucking me, but the real trip for him was bursting the bubble of my dream world afterward. He got a kick out of humiliating me. There wouldn't be another summons to late-night meetings at the field house. That was all right. Who needed that miserable excuse for a human being, anyway? I did, that's who. I slipped into an uneasy coma with that thought in mind.

I woke Saturday morning with an erection that was something more than a piss-hard. Resisting the temptation to relive the previous night, I cleaned up, did my homework and headed for the swimming pool. A block from my place I saw Rory Mason traipsing along. He accepted my offer of a ride, and as he slid his butt into the seat, I recalled he'd seen me with a boner at the game last night. I promptly achieved another one. Rory didn't seem to notice. Shit! I was going for it.

"What's up?"

"We're going for a ride," I announced just the way Rex would have. "Downtown. To the Palacio."

That didn't bring a reaction. Maybe he didn't know about the glory hole. It was quiet in the car until I parked as close to the hotel as I could get.

"Let's go to the men's room."

"I don't need to go."

I rounded on him. "Yeah. You do. There's a big glory hole in there, and you're going to take care of this bone I've got." I fingered my rapidly growing cock through my jeans.

"Geez, Toby," he sort of wheezed.

"What's the matter, you've never seen a guy's cock?"

"Not...not like *that!*"

"Well, you're going to get a better look at it."

"I don't think so. Not...not down there."

"How do you know the men's room is downstairs?"

"Everybody does."

"You ever stick your cock through the hole?"

He swallowed and shook his head.

"You ever suck one through it?"

An emphatic shake of the head this time.

"Well, you're gonna suck this one. Right now."

"I don't like it down there. If...if you want me to jack you off or something, we can go to the West Mesa. Or your apartment."

"Uh-uh. Come on. Stop stalling. You've been sniffing around, now you're going to get it."

"Not down there," he said again.

I cuffed him on the ear. "Get out of the car, Rory."

His hand flew to his ear. "Don't do that. Don't hit me, man."

"I'll hit you whenever I want, asshole," I said in my best Rex tones. "Now come on."

I have no idea why I wanted to go to the dank, smelly men's room in the basement. Rory was right. My apartment would have been a better place. Maybe it was because I wanted to experience what Rex had felt as he bucked up against the wall while I swallowed his cock and his cum.

I got out of the car and walked down the stairs, never once looking back. I knew he'd follow me. No question. Once inside the bathroom, I made sure no one was there and shoved him in the far stall. I took the one Rex had used.

I played it like he had. I stood as if I were going to take a leak and unbuttoned my trousers to pull out my cock. Unlike his, mine was already hard, hot and pulsing. I stepped back against the far wall and slipped my trousers down to my ankles, giving whoever was on the other side a good look at my cock. To me, at that moment, it wasn't Rory over there...it was someone else. It was Rex looking at me through that hole, wanting me, waiting for me. I stepped up and put just the tip of it through the hole, just as he had done.

At first, nothing. Then I felt a warm tongue caress the slit. I pushed more of me through. Lips closed over my cock. Then I shoved my hips, driving myself down the waiting throat. And then *I was* Rex. I thrust hard against the wooden wall, pushing my cock into Rex's mouth. *Rex sucking Rex. Rex fucking Rex's mouth.* Losing control, I bucked and humped and tried to crawl right through the wall into the other booth. I pulled out, I shoved it back in, I fucked like a madman, grunting and groaning, banging against the wall, making scuffling noises as my shoes fought to give me traction for my assault.

And then it happened. I came. I shot. Every nerve in my body went screwy, and I got that electric charge as I unloaded. It was the best fucking orgasm I'd ever had, and that included the one when the *real* Rex had his big cock up my ass. When I came down off my high, I pulled out and bent to pull up my pants, almost falling, my knees were so rubbery.

Still panting, I opened the door and was surprised to find a man standing there.

"You really get it on, kid. Maybe we ought to get together sometime."

I ignored him and banged on the stall door. "Come on, Rory. Let's go."

"I...I can't come out. There's somebody there."

"Get the fuck out here, or I'll whip your ass," I snarled.

The stall door opened, and Rory darted past us and out of the men's room.

"Wow!" the stranger, a man probably in his thirties said. "I'd sure like to be the meat between that sandwich."

"Three's a crowd," I said as I marched out.

As I knew he would be, Rory was waiting for me beside my car. I unlocked the door without saying a word. I got in the driver's seat and pulled out onto the street. Now that I'd calmed down, I wondered how Rory felt about what we'd done?

"You've got a nice body," he whispered timidly "You're handsome, Toby. Best-looking boy on campus." I must have shown my surprise because he came up to look me in the eye. "You are. Really!"

"What about Rex Lundgren?"

"He's handsome, too, but like a picture. You're handsome like somebody real. I'll do it for you again, but I won't do it for anybody else."

"You better not, you little pussy." Why was I getting huffy with him again? "And stay away from Rex Fucking Lundgren, you hear?"

He nodded, a hurt look on his face.

Strangely exhilarated and slightly ashamed of the way I was treating him, I couldn't help keeping it up.

"Next time, I'm going to fuck your ass. What do you say to that?"

"Not...not in the Palacio."

"Naw. I'm through with that now. Next time there's not going to be a wall between us. It's just going to be pecker to butthole. What do you say to that?"

"Will it hurt?"

"Some. But when you bust your balls with my cock up your ass, you'll think you've gone to heaven."

"If you say so, Toby."

I pulled up in front of his place, but didn't kill the motor. "Get out of here, you little fag. And when I call you, you better come, you hear? Do we understand one another?"

He swallowed and studied the floorboard. "Yes. But...why are you being so mean? I did what you wanted, didn't I?"

"Yeah, and you'll do it again whenever I want. But right now, the sight of your pasty face makes me sick!"

I watched him walk away. What was the matter with me? I didn't really want him to go. Shit, I'd like to play a game of chess or something, but I couldn't help myself. I'd found a powerful new emotion. Not sex. Not lust, but bullying. For once in my life, it was me pushing somebody else around! And I fucking *loved* it. Just like I was going to love fucking that trim ass.

But before that, I might just go back and try to find that good-looking man at the Palacio. That fucking glory hole was calling me back.

THREE WEEKS IN
THE CEMETERY

Shaun Levin

1

The sun filters through the leaves and the silence is complete. It's my first time here. I came in through the High Street entrance past a group of drunks sunning themselves on the grass in the forecourt. I've crossed the cemetery to its far end, to a bench on the path by the wall that flanks Bouverie Road. This is Abney Park Cemetery. Home to William Booth, father of the Salvation Army, and to gay men looking for love. The guidebook says: *No other cemetery has been better served in English literature.* I'm on my summer holidays, in a new flat, in another part of London.

The sun has turned the treetops to lace. The breeze flips over leaves on the path, changing them from emerald to dusty green. I'm here on a bench with my sketchbook by a grave with plastic poppies. There's a man coming toward me, reading a book. He stops and the tension mounts; his well-trained eye sizes me up.

"Have you got the time?" he says.

Clichés that open up possibilities.

"It must be around noon," I say.

He sits down on the bench beside me, feigning interest in my sketches, telling me he'd always wanted to be a painter. He's sweaty from walking around the cemetery for hours.

"It is hot," I say.

"Can you make me hotter?" he says, tucking his hand under my sketch-pad.

He cups my cock and balls in his fist and grins at me.

"It's not that big," I say.

"It's big enough for me," he says.

I show him pictures of the cemetery in the guidebook. We talk about living in London. He's in exile from Europe; I left Africa as a boy and have never been back. We kiss and lick each other and I pinch the tips of his nipples with my nails.

"Come fuck me in the bushes," he says.

"I've got a place just down the road," I say.

"But I don't know you," he says.

"We'll just fuck," I say. "It's not like I'm going to kill you."

We leave the cemetery laughing, holding hands as if we're lovers. We buy apple juice from Harvest Wines and fat purple grapes from the grocers by the funeral parlor. By the time we get home I know everything I'll ever know about him. Except one story. He tells me enough names, dates and places to explain how he could lie back on a stranger's bed, stretch open his arse-hole and say: "Look, just like a pussy; stick your finger in." As for me, after two years of celibacy, after twenty-four months of nothing, just work and paying the rent and lots of dope-smoking in my room, alone, my show is back on the road.

"Are you sure you've fist-fucked before?" he says.

In the silence after we come, lying next to him, I stroke the down on the cheeks of his arse and I run the tips of my fingers along his spine.

"Do you have to work tomorrow?" I say.

"I must go home soon," he says.

"You can stay if you like," I say.

"I need to go," he says. "It doesn't mean I won't see you again."

The sweat has dried on my skin and I pull the duvet up from the foot of the bed. He writes his name and number on a piece of paper. I say what I say, and he tells me one last story.

2

In the cemetery, behind the derelict chapel, there's a patch of lawn with a bench. That's where I am today. The solitude and green are beautiful. The guidebook says: *In the spring and early summer, the rich variety of birdsong adds to the cemetery's idyllic woodland aura.* It's true. The wind in the leaves, like waves, drowns out all other sounds. This is tranquillity. Until a man sits down on the grass in front of me and takes off his shirt. An onionskin of sweat covers his body and his nipples are dark brown. I can't imagine doing anything gentle to him.

He has the body of an American porn star. He tucks his T-shirt into his back pocket. His cock has left a permanent outline on the fabric of his jeans. What seems like fat is only resting muscle; his skin is browned from being half naked whenever he can—walking home from the gym, sitting on an old chair in his overgrown back garden, cruising this cemetery for hours to ensure every man has sucked his cock and massaged his pumped-up tits.

I'll do anything to be next.

My sketch-pad becomes a prayer book as I slide off the bench onto my knees. How can men have such perfect bodies? I must draw him, put him into words, imprint every pore and hair of his onto my senses. My mouth is dry. He smoothes his palm across his chest. His nipples darken like an invitation. The chapel's stained-glass windows begin to crack like sugar and crash to the ground. The choir sings deafening hosannas. Jesus howls and rips the rusting nails from his aching flesh. Ecstasy is loosed upon the world.

The American porn star moves to sit on a fallen tombstone by the running water near the main path, his body catching the sunlight. I can tell he's a regular in the cemetery and in demand; the kind of man men notice. The kind of man who can pick and choose. I carry on drawing—it's the only way I know how to attract love. Sometimes it works. The porn star lights a cigarette. Does he know I can bring him voluptuous pleasure? Is he aware of the wondrous things I've done with my penis?

He splashes water into his hair. The strip of sun between the chapel and treetops has narrowed; still, there's room for him to walk toward me, remove his shoes and jeans and lie naked in the grass, his skin exposed and welcoming.

And the man from last time? He handed me the bit of paper with his name, and I said: Is that a Jewish name? So he told me a story: His grandmother and grandfather owned a traveling theater company in the 1920s and '30s. He was German, she was French, and when the war came the grandfather joined the Nazi party, which meant they got invited to perform for SS officers. They traveled between concentration camps, performing Moliére. When they realized what was going on beyond the officers' quarters, his grandfather began to hide Jews and Gypsies amongst the ball gowns in their caravans and drive them out to the partisans in the woods. Some lived to tell the tale, but the French still see his family as collaborators.

* * *

The porn star's name is Henrik and he's Denmark's number-one rock star; a sex-crazed six-foot-two man with jet-black hair who comes to London for the kind and quantity of sex he wants. Once a year he is a regular in the cemetery. He smiles without fear and walks like a man who has never been lost. He rests his back against the chapel wall while I suck his cock, his thick pubes damp with sweat and someone else's cum; leaning over, almost kissing the top of my head, he dribbles spit onto the root of his cock for me to wet my lips with. He wants to be fucked out in the open. So while I'm inside him, fucking him from behind, watching my cock go in and out of his hairless arsehole, he answers all my questions. That's what made me love him. He knew I could be trusted.

The cemetery gates are locked by the time we're done, so we climb through a hole in the fence by the timber yard and go for a drink at Bar Lorca, a straight pickup joint on Church Street. I get us drinks from the bar, half expecting him not to be there when I turn round.

"I'm going to be in *Hamlet*, the musical," he says.

"Are you Hamlet?" I say.

"Yes," he says. "What do you do?" (Hadn't I told him in the cemetery?)

"I'm a painter," I say.

"I paint sometimes," he says. "I spend two or three days painting and when I go out again I feel like the loneliest man in the world."

"That's how I feel most days," I say.

When they call for last orders I suggest we go for coffee. And each time he agrees I feel braver, like a god-fearing Christian in the lion's den, charming the beast with divine encouragement. We buy coffee at the kebab house and walk down Church

Street, stopping to look at children's clothes in the window of a secondhand shop. He leans in toward me, thinking I wanted to whisper in his ear, me thinking he wants to be kissed.

"I don't think I can return that kiss," he says.

"I didn't think you would," I say, the lion's claw-marks across my cheek.

"I'm just tired of quick sex," he says. "I've had a boyfriend for nine years."

"I've only had sex twice in the past two years," I say. "And last week was the first time."

"You're not looking for quick sex," he says. "You're looking for someone to love."

I walk him to Defoe Cabs because he wants to go to Heaven and I have to get up early. I have things to do. He leaves without giving me his phone number; we make no plans to meet up again, but I am a Rottweiler when it comes to love: I call the Danish Tourist Board and get them to send me information about all the musicals in Copenhagen.

On the day of the première I send him flowers with a post-card of an angel on a tomb in Abney Park Cemetery. His call comes two days later.

"Thank you for the flowers," he says.

"Do you like them?" I say.

"Can I see you when I come to London next time?" he says.

3

The educational aspects of cemeteries, the guidebook says, *were strong at Abney Park, where trees and shrubs were labeled for the enlightenment of all those who walked there.* Midsummer, school holidays, temperatures soaring and I'm back here on a bench shaded by trees, cherishing each little breeze as if it were a lover's breath. I watch a man walking along a path in just shorts and a rucksack. A couple—a man and a woman—walk past me, saying things like: "I hadn't spoken to her in seven years, and then there she was, on the phone, babbling on about some wedding she was off to in Scotland."

Another man appears from the opposite end of the path, on his bicycle. And despite Henrik, despite the anticipation of his return, our emails, I feel this great sense of elation when the man on the bicycle slows down and dismounts. He comes closer, a strawberry-blond angel with a sprinkling of light brown hair on his chest.

It is always a great shock at moments of heightened passion when others appear on the scene: three chatty men walking their bicycles, as if exercising ponies, speaking French, stopping to read plaques under the trees. And I want to follow, to tell them I too have a bicycle, I too love to saunter in the company of friends, I too can chat in French, if they'll be patient with me.

I walk toward the man who is an angel. My mouth dried by fear that my voice will squeak. I keep all sounds in the back of my throat and I say: "Hi." And he says: "Hi." And I say: "What are you up to?" And he says: "Cycling around. You?"

"I don't know," I say. "Just sketching."

While we talk he dislodges his cock from his shorts, like a finger puppet, squeezing the pink head out of its foreskin, coaxing it.

"Do you want to go for a walk?" I say.

He stops at the opening of a path and leads us into the bushes, leans his bicycle against a tree, faces me and, literally, drops his shorts.

"That was quick," I say.

His lips are soft. The noises he makes are the sound of unexpected and accurate pleasuring; the sound one makes when one feels deliciously weak and vulnerable. We are strangers in a forest jerking ourselves off. His eyes are blue and his skin taut and hairless. He says he'd like to see me again, that I look like the serious type. I tell him to keep flicking his fingers like that over the tips of my nipples. I come into my hand and offer it to him to drink. He wiggles his tongue over my open palm, as if what I was offering might burn him, then licks it and groans. I wipe his cum off my thigh with a tissue and throw it into the bushes. We smile. It's exhilarating.

NEW YORK'S
PHYNEST

Donald Peebles Jr.

Jesse Foster walked down the stairs at the 59th Street/ Columbus Circle subway station, leading to the platform for the Downtown A, B, C and D trains. He sashayed over to the newsstand like the regal African-Native American queen he knew he was. He thought about purchasing the latest issue of *Sister 2 Sister Magazine* with his favorite television gossip personality host Wendy Williams on the cover. Since it looked like it was going to take a while for the next D train he needed to arrive, he faced the fiftysomething Middle Eastern owner to request the magazine and a king-size Snickers bar to satisfy him. He pulled six singles out of his black leather wallet to give to the owner, received some change back, and gave thanks for the magazine and Snickers bar.

Not having anything in his stomach since the seven Rosemary and Olive Oil–flavored Triscuits he ate four hours before, he decided to take a bite of his king-size Snickers bar. He always loved the milk-chocolate sweetness, caramel ecstasy, nougat bliss and salty peanut kink in his mouth. He savored it like it was a nine-inch, veined black dick, which he hadn't had in his mouth and badookadunk for two years. As he chewed the last chunk of his Snickers bar, he closed his eyes with the knowledge of chocolate's aphrodisiac powers on every fiber of his being.

He turned his pink Apple IPod Shuffle on to play Janet Jackson's "Feedback." As far as he was concerned as a proud gay man, the music was shady as fuck. He enjoyed shaking his ass at Nathan Hale Williams and Yamil X's Ocean Wednesday night parties at Splash. He loved showing the African-American, Caribbean, and Latino boyz he had the moves of his African and Native American ancestors. They couldn't take their eyes off him since he lost 115 pounds of emotional-eating fat. He bedazzled them with his curly black 'fro, dark-brown eyes, deep-set eyebrows, broad nose, thick seductive brown-pink lips, Debbi Morgan dimples, thin yet built 185-pound body and a round badookadunk. However, he didn't want another queen to bump pocketbooks and patties with. It wouldn't have been a good look.

As soon as Janet tore it up, Jesse couldn't help but to shake his ass on the subway platform. The newsstand owner found himself amused as did some of the straphangers who waited for whichever trains they needed. He moved his body with lots of carefree abandon. They would've never thought he was an aspiring backup dancer who wanted to dance for Janet. When "Feedback" concluded on his IPod Shuffle, he looked around in amazement to see the newsstand owner and straphangers applauding for him. Some of the straphangers walked up to him and handed him dollar bills. He refused all of their handouts, letting them know he wasn't a subway performer but thanked all of them for their enthusiasm. As soon as the Downtown D train pulled into the station and he was about to get onto it, Jesse was stopped abruptly by the feel of someone's hands tapping his shoulder.

"Yo! Get your hands off me!" Jesse yelled.

"I don't mean you any harm, my brother," the African-American police officer replied in a raspy voice. "I believe you dropped something."

Not only couldn't Jesse believe he'd nearly blown off the police officer's head but he had nearly lost his Apple IPod Shuffle. "I feel like an idiot. Can you ever forgive me, Officer?" he asked, not wanting to be arrested over bullshit.

"Hey, don't sweat over the small stuff," the officer smiled.

Jesse stood in the middle of one of the train doors, completely transfixed over him. He was used to seeing out-of-shape police officers trying to chase and shoot various people in his neighborhood of South Jamaica, Queens. He found it hilarious to see them stopping either at Dunkin Donuts or Mickey Ds, piling on extra unnecessary girth. Yet the officer standing in front of him didn't fit his physical perceptions of police officers. The police officer was a dark-brown-skinned brother with a shiny baldy; dark, deep-set eyebrows; honey-glazed eyes; a broad nose; a neatly-trimmed goatee; thick brown lips and perfect white teeth. He had the massive build of a defensive linebacker on an NFL team, weighing 255 pounds solid and standing at five eleven. It was obvious he worked out at the gym five days a week, performing both cardio and circuit-training workouts whenever he was off-duty as a civilian. If someone ever asked Jesse a year before if he was attracted to cops, his answer would've been no. Considering the police officer standing in front of him was a rare specimen of New York's Phynest, he quickly changed his mind in a heartbeat. As far as he was concerned, New York's Phynest could protect and serve him any time and any place.

When the computerized conductor called for everyone to

stand clear of the doors, Jesse and New York's Phynest quickly stepped back onto the platform. The Downtown D train pulled off and departed out of the station.

"I didn't mean for you to miss your train, my brother," New York's Phynest apologized.

"That's all right. If it weren't for you letting me know I dropped my IPod Shuffle, I would've lost it and then had to walk to the Apple Store on Fifth Avenue to get a replacement. You saved me a trip. Thank you, Officer," he replied.

"You're more than welcome. By the way, my name is Officer Jacob Williams."

"Mine is Jesse Foster."

"It's nice to meet you. I must confess something right now."

"What is it?"

Officer Williams looked around to see if the coast was clear. Realizing the coast was clear, he inched his face close to Jesse's. "I was checking you out, shaking dat ass of yours," he confessed, relieved it was off his chest.

Jesse smiled at the fact he wasn't going to get arrested for causing a public disturbance. "How was I?" he wondered.

"You have the makings of a professional dancer. You got mad skills, Jesse," he replied with sincerity.

"Thank you, Officer Williams," he said, appreciating the positive compliments.

"I want to ask you this. How many songs does this little IPod hold? I've never seen an IPod this small."

"My pink IPod Shuffle is supposed to hold up to five hundred songs. Since I have mostly underground soulful house music and their songs can be pretty long, it holds around three-hundred and twenty-five songs. This is convenient whenever I'm doing cardio at the gym or taking a long stroll wherever I happen to be," Jesse said, and laughed, with a slight nod.

As soon as Officer Williams got ready to reply, a White or Latino twink stopped in front of them. "Excuse me, Officer! I would like to know what train I need to take to West 4th Street," he inquired with timidity.

Oh, I don't believe this shit. As soon as I get play from New York's Phynest, here comes this mealy mouth tramp trying to prevent me from getting some dick. He knows how to get to the fuckin' Village. He needs to know New York's Phynest is mine so he can go to Christopher Street and turn tricks for someone else, Jesse thought to himself, rolling his eyes and sucking his teeth.

"Young man, you can take any one of these trains on these tracks to get to West 4th Street," Officer Williams directed.

"Thank you, Officer," the twink cooed with a soap opera–diva grin.

"What a fuckin' shady bitch," Jesse mumbled, crossing his arms together.

"Did you say something, Jesse?" Officer Williams asked as the A train arrived at the station.

"No, I didn't say anything," Jesse lied, relieved to see the twink disappear into the crowd getting on the train. *I know New York Phynest better give me his digits because Miss Honey got to get home to watch my SoapNet. I'm not some sideline ho waiting for dick,* he thought to himself.

"What were we talking about before?" Officer Williams asked, making an effort to get closer to Jesse. However, when Jesse was about to answer his question, he recognized a colleague of his approaching them. "What's up, Martinez? What're you doing here? I'd thought you would be patrolling the nightwalkers over there in Central Park."

"Very funny, Williams," Officer Martinez laughed, giving him a pound. "I suppose you're here to fulfill your year-end quota of making the most arrests of New York straphanger pussy."

Ooo damn, Jesse thought to himself, echoing his favorite line from Electrik Red's "So Good." While he thought Officer Claudio Martinez had such a dirty mouth, what was he going to do about it? Absolutely nothing! There was something about him that awakened his curiosity. He couldn't help but admire his stocky yet muscular physique. He was a brown-skinned Dominican who stood at five eleven and weighed 280 pounds. He had dark eyebrows, dark-brown eyes, a broad nose, thick pink-brown lips and a jovial smile like Sammy Sosa. Unlike Sammy, he was extremely proud of his African roots and didn't give a fuck if some of his fellow Dominicans had a problem with it. As far as he was concerned, he was an Afro-Dominican, so they had to deal with it. Jesse could tell he worked out five times a week at the gym like Officer Williams. He imagined him to be a beast in the bed with a fat and thick dick, making the sisters scream, moan, cream and come.

"You got jokes," Officer Williams laughed, snapping Jesse out of his daze.

"I can't stand here to watch you charm all and I mean ALL of New York's eligible bachelorette and married pussy. I got to go see if I can bring home some pussy to my bachelor pad. You wish you were that lucky, Williams, since you got to report home to the wife," Officer Martinez said.

What the fuck? No, Officer Martinez gotta be kidding, Jesse thought to himself.

"Yeah, thanks for fuckin' reminding me, Martinez. I've been with the wife for ten years and I'm not going to mess that up by being sloppy with the pussy. She caught me messing around many times behind her back. She threatened to leave me and take me off her medical insurance," Officer Williams confirmed.

"Since my shift is almost done, I'm going to head back to the precinct, push out, and head home for some after-work pussy."

"I'll check with you later, Martinez."

"Peace in the Middle East, Williams."

Officer Martinez walked away with his cock-of-the-walk swaggalito, causing Officer Williams to nod his head with his "He's so crazee!" facial expression. He turned his gaze back to Jesse's clearly perturbed face. "What's wrong, Jesse? Are you okay?" he asked.

Jesse produced his fierce sista girl stare at him. By the time he began to reply, he noticed two middle-aged African-American, female MTA maintenance employees walking toward Officer Williams. *I don't fuckin' believe this shit. Roseanne and Jackie have to ruin this. He's supposed to be my booty call,* he thought to himself.

Officer Williams turned to face Jesse with an apologetic look. "I'm sorry, but we're going to have to cut our conversation short," he said.

Jesse rolled his eyes and sucked his teeth. "Whatever! I'm outta here. It's been a total waste of time," he snapped as the D train quickly pulled into the station. As soon as the train door opened, he got in and stood there looking fierce. When the computerized conductor called for everyone to stand clear of the doors, Jesse gave a dirty look at Officer Williams as the train left the station.

By the time Jesse reached the Seventh Avenue subway station to transfer onto the Uptown/Queens E train, he looked in his mud cloth shoulder bag for his pink IPod Shuffle. He couldn't seem to locate it, so he checked in both of his brown coat pockets. Nothing, so he quickly walked over to the bench where he emptied his bag out. Papers, personal mail, pens, and peppermint balls fell all over the bench, but to no avail; his pink IPod Shuffle was nowhere to be found.

"Fuck!" he yelled, not caring if the other straphangers heard him or not. "I have no fuckin' choice but to see if New York's Phynest is still at 59th Street/Columbus Circle, talking to Roseanne and Jackie."

He placed all of his stuff back into his bag and walked across the platform to wait for an Uptown/Bronx B or D train to arrive. When it did, he rushed inside. Five minutes later, he got off directly in front of the Middle Eastern newsstand owner. Hoping Officer Williams gave him the IPod Shuffle, he approached him. "Excuse me, sir! I want to know if the police officer is still here in the station," he asked.

"I'm sorry, but he already left, my friend," the Middle Eastern newsstand owner replied, shrugging.

"Thank you!" Jesse said with disappointment in his voice, walking toward one of the exits. As soon as he finally arrived on the Central Park side of the station, he was relieved by the fresh night air. Out of the blue, he felt someone's rough hand squeeze one arm while a gun poked the other.

"Just do what I say and there won't be any fuckin' trouble," the gunman warned.

Jesse wasn't that stupid to risk getting shot and killed, especially when someone held a gun on him. He felt he had no choice but to do what was instructed.

The gunman blindfolded Jesse's eyes and tied his wrists with long strands of black duct tape. "Get inside the car!" he ordered, holding the gun on Jesse's shivering back.

Jesse did as he was told, scooting his badookadunk onto the backseat of a black car. He heard the door shut when the gunman sat next to him with his gun.

"Let's do this!" the gunman said to the driver, whose face was also masked.

The car quickly drove into the 59th Street entrance of Central

Park, passing the joggers who were on their way out; the park was pitch-black with the exception of the streetlights.

The car stopped at the 103rd Street route while the gunman held on to Jesse and pulled him from the car. The driver placed the lock signal on and shut the door immediately. Seeing the coast was clear, they walked into the bushes. Jesse had no idea where they were taking him but knew to keep his cool. He wasn't trying to turn into a statistic whose murder wouldn't make it onto the ten o'clock news.

After a five-minute walk into the bushes, the gunman and the driver stopped. Jesse wondered what was happening amid the mysterious silence. Suddenly, his mind seemed to play tricks on him. While the duct tape was removed from his eyes and wrists, the gun was still secured to his back. An unexpected sensation overcame every fiber of his being when the gunman rested his gloved hand on Jesse's bulge. Satisfied, the gunman started to undress Jesse. He felt a little breeze, standing there in nothing but his black boxer briefs. He heard the driver's groaning sounds as he unzipped his pants and allowed them to fall down to his ankles. The driver rescued his dick from the imprisonment of his tighty whities and jerked it back and forth in a slow rhythmic motion. It became inevitable to Jesse that the gunman was going to roll his black boxer briefs down and off his legs. When they were stripped off his maleness, he didn't know what to think next. *Oooh child, things are going to get freakier*, he thought to himself.

Seeing the driver's well-endowed ten inches of dark-brown dick, the gunman inched close to Jesse's right ear. "Go over there and suck his dick nice and slow," he whispered, squeezing, smacking and slapping Jesse's ass.

The gunman walked Jesse over to the driver, whose dick was ready and erect. Jesse didn't expect the driver to slop his dark-brown, ten-inch dick into his mouth so quickly. He couldn't believe how long it was yet he adapted to the driver face-fucking him. He closed his eyes to imagine chewing on a king-size Snickers bar with its milk-chocolate sweetness, caramel ecstasy, nougat bliss and salty peanut kink. He licked the brown dickhead all around, absorbing some precum for some extra flavor. He trailed his mouth all the way to his pubic area. Seeing how Jesse's mouth colonized the driver's dick turned the gunman on. Since it seemed Jesse wasn't scared of the dick, the gunman finally released the gun's grip off Jesse's back and dropped it to the ground. The gunman spread Jesse's asscheeks apart and quickly dug his face into his warm crevice. Jesse's body shook a wee bit, loving the tender yet aggressive feel of the gunman's pink tongue tasting his timeless treasures. The gunman's mouth nibbled and grabbed ahold of Jesse's moist, pink-brownish delights. He seemed to enjoy hearing Jesse moan in ecstasy. His mouth got all greedy for Jesse's ass, slurping his wet tongue in and around his hole. Jesse couldn't help but close his eyes. The gunman's tongue made him feel open and loose. He pushed his ass way deep into the gunman's face. It got the gunman so hot, he placed a finger into Jesse's hole, circled it for a few seconds, took it out and licked it. He got off his knees and slapped Jesse's ass.

Jesse stood there while the gunman whispered something into the driver's ear. "I think it's time to come clean with him since we got him open and loose."

"Are you sure?"

"Shit, from the way he's been sucking that dick of yours and the way his fat brown ass is creaming, he is ready, willing and able to know we're going to give him a night to remember."

Jesse sensed the gunman's voice sounded very familiar but couldn't quite put a finger on it.

"All right, let's get some of this good-ass boy-pussy."

Oh shit! I knew his voice sounded familiar. It's Officer Martinez with his dirty mouth! Jesse thought to himself, feeling his ass being lubed up.

The gunman walked in front of Jesse and pulled his mask off his face.

"It is you, Officer Martinez!" Jesse said, finally receiving his confirmation. "Since you're here, then the driver has to be..."

"Officer Williams is here in da house," the driver revealed, pulling off his own mask.

Jesse nodded his head in amazement. "You mean to tell me you two kidnapped me just to get some ass? Oh, please, if that was all you two wanted, you could've just told me. I wanted to give it up to you two tonight when we were at the 59th Street/Columbus Circle subway station."

"Is that a fact, Jesse?" Officer Williams inquired.

"Yes! You should know since your big dick was so fuckin' tasty in my mouth. Why don't we continue where we left off, New York's Phynest?" Jesse cooed.

"All right, let's do this shit!" Officers Williams and Martinez agreed in unison.

Officer Martinez got in front of Jesse, who finally got the chance to have the other officer's dick in his anticipating mouth. It was fat and thick as he imagined like a real ripe platano. His mouth gulped it for dear life. He figured he was packing ten inches of brown-skinned Dominican-style platano. He licked and sucked his pink dickhead that was like a cherry Charms Blow-Pop with its sweet and satisfying taste. His tongue trailed along the size of his shaft, giving his mouth ample permission to engulf the totality of the officer's machismo. He looked up to witness the pure delight of Officer Martinez, who couldn't believe it when Jesse began licking, sucking and savoring his huge nut sac.

Officer Williams's long ten inches glided easily into Jesse's ass. He held his hands on Jesse's ass firmly as he pumped rapidly. His dick attacked Jesse's boy-pussy walls with a fury. He occasionally teased him by pulling out and pushing in again. Figuring how moist and dripping Jesse's asshole became, he pulled out completely and jammed it all the way into his ass to the point where his nuts clung against Jesse's opening. He sank deeper into Jesse's ass. He didn't want to come when Jesse pushed his ass against his dick, making it a perfect combination.

Officer Martinez released Jesse's grip and pulled his brown platano dick out of his mouth and smacked his face playfully with it. Officer Williams gently eased his dick out of Jesse's ass.

Jesse couldn't believe it when they finally stripped out of their police uniforms. *Fuck, where were they when I dialed 9-1-1 to protect and serve my neighborhood?* He was so in awe of their stocky yet muscular physiques with their juicy chests, abs of steel, six-packs of thunder, big good dicks, and tree-trunk legs.

Officer Martinez lay on the ground while Jesse climbed over him. Jesse positioned his ass over Officer Martinez's fat and thick dick. He maneuvered it to his comfort zone, lowering his badookadunk completely, and enacted colonial rule on the prized platano. Just as Jesse set forth to ride and gallop on the ten-incher, the impossible happened. It was absolutely incredible when Officer Williams sneaked his dick into Jesse's ass. Since he was an aspiring backup dancer, Jesse knew he could be anally eased by them at the same time. Their big dicks double-filled his ass and collided with each other. Officer Martinez rapidly thrust his dick, causing Jesse to shudder like his white-hot lava was going to erupt from his volcano. Officer Williams pumped voraciously while the trilingual moans and groans of Ebonics, Dominicanish and Pig Latin dominated the night air in Central Park. Sweat glistened all over their bodies. The two dicks fought for anal domination once and for all as Officer Martinez pumped his dick rapidly and fully into Jesse's ass. Officer Williams tried to knock him out of the box until they decided to take turns. They did just that and everything went smooth sailing. After fifteen minutes, Officer Williams shook, pulled out and stood in front of Jesse. Officer Martinez shook and tapped the side of Jesse's ass as a signal for him to get off his dick. Jesse quickly leaped off when they ordered him to kneel before them. They yelled like madmen as they positioned their dicks at Jesse's mouth. Jesse's eager pink tongue lapped up their creamy wads of thick white cum that tasted sweet with apple and orange juice flavorings. Officer Martinez held Jesse's face as Officer Williams jammed his entire dick inside his mouth, making sure he drank all of his chocolate cream. Officer Williams switched places with Officer Martinez, whose fat platano dick deposited all of his nectar to the back of Jesse's throat. Satisfied, Officer Martinez pulled his dick out of Jesse's mouth and Officer Williams released his grip on Jesse.

"Damn, Williams! That was some good ass. I can go home now and sleep much easier tonight," Officer Martinez laughed.

"Yeah, the nut has been sucked and fucked out of me for real, Martinez."

"Let's get the fuck outta Central Park before someone sees us."

The trio quickly gathered their clothes off the ground, put them on, made sure any evidence wasn't left behind, got into the car and jetted the hell back to the 59th Street/Columbus Circle subway station.

A few minutes later, Officers Williams and Martinez dropped Jesse off at the station. By the time Jesse had nearly disappeared underground, Officer Williams got out of the driver's seat.

"Wait a minute, Jesse! I think you're forgetting something," he called out.

"I don't think I am," Jesse said.

"This belongs to you," Officer Williams stated, handing Jesse his pink Apple IPod Shuffle.

"Oh shit! I thought I lost this forever. Thank you. I don't know what to say."

"There's nothing to say. We're just doing our job."

"That's right, Jesse, but if there's anything you need from Martinez or me, please feel free to stop by at the Midtown North Precinct right there on West 54th Street between Eighth and Ninth Avenues."

"I will."

"Get home safe," Officer Martinez said.

"You too, Officer Martinez."

"Bye!" Jesse called out, walking away into the train station.

While Officers Williams and Martinez drove away to their respective homes for the night, Jesse waited once again for the Downtown D train. *If I ever knew there were phyne-ass Black and Latino cops who were handsome like those two, I would get myself arrested every day,* he thought, turning on his IPod Shuffle to listen to Janet Jackson's "Feedback."

JONAH AND THE WHALE

Aaron Travis

Jonah: Five feet, seven inches of lean young muscle attached to a wide-open mouth that's always hungry. Bright blue eyes, curly black hair. A pair of snow-white buns covered with silky peach fuzz, a sturdy little dick that stands up bone hard at the very thought of taking my cock down his throat....

I met him one night this summer at a dirty bookstore near campus, cruising the peep show. I could peg his type right away. Young, eager, reckless. The original cock-hungry kid. A real dick-hound. The kind who checks out a guy's crotch first and may never even get around to looking at his face.

I spotted him right away. And he spotted me—fixing his bright blue eyes on the bulge in my jeans, staring and licking his lips. If looks could burn, my pants would've been singed to a cinder in two seconds flat.

I decided to tease him a little first. Let it build. Play hard to get. I pretended I didn't even see him standing there across the aisle, drooling and staring at my box. He was too shy to just come up and ask for it—probably used to older, more experienced guys like me taking the lead. Instead I just stood there, arms crossed, feeling my cock stiffen and throb down my pants leg, pretending to be bored and waiting for something interesting to come along.

It was late Saturday night, about closing time for the bars. The arcade was already busy and got busier. Plenty of guys were giving Jonah the cruise, but Jonah had eyes only for me. He kept his place, mooning and pouting and fidgeting, stealing furtive glances at my face when he wasn't staring outright at my crotch.

Finally it got to be too much for him. His patience snapped. His appetite got the best of him. Jonah tore himself away, and for the next two hours I watched him indiscriminately enter booth after booth with just about every man who came along.

He'd disappear through a thin wooden door—catching my eye just before it closed—and for the next fifteen minutes I'd hear the muffled sounds of sucking, gagging, groans of pleasure. I didn't need X-ray vision to see the situation inside. The sucking and gagging came from Jonah. The groans were from the man he was pleasing.

Eventually the door would rattle and open. Jonah's trick would step out first, adjusting his pants, smiling sheepishly, satisfied and heading for the exit. And then Jonah would emerge, looking a little shamefaced, head bowed—his eyes, as always, at crotch-level. Glancing up just long enough to catch my eye and reestablish contact. I'd give him a faint sneer and turn away in mock-disgust. Jonah would bite his lip, looking disappointed and stubborn and defiant all at the same time. Then go after his next meal. The boy was desperate to suck.

I finally got disgusted for real when he entered a booth with his last trick, a grossly obese, balding old guy in a rumpled suit, some drunken professor-type from the campus across the street.

From the look Jonah gave me just as the door was closing, I got the idea he was doing it just to get at me somehow, showing me how low he'd go. For the next half hour I had to listen to the fat guy huffing and puffing and making little squealing sounds inside the booth. I started to burn—imagining Jonah down on his knees, opening wide for a guy like that, giving his mouth to any man who'd show him a hard cock.

Finally the big guy came—whinnying like a horse and shaking so hard he rattled the whole row of booths. The cruisers lined up and down the aisle glanced at each other and smirked. A few seconds later the door opened and the fat professor squeezed out, wiping the sweat off his forehead and wearing a smug leer on his face, knowing he'd scored way out of his league and cock-proud of it, strutting for the rest of the cruisers. A bunch of guys headed for the open booth, but I beat them to the punch.

Jonah was just stepping out. I blocked him and forced him back inside, slamming the thin door behind me. I like teasing guys; I don't like being teased in return. He looked startled, maybe even a little scared. He flinched when I reached up and grabbed his face, but he didn't try to stop me.

I ran my middle finger around his lips, smooth and shiny with something more than spit. I squeezed his jaw to force his mouth open and slid my finger inside. I could feel the stuff on his tongue, slippery and slick.

"You've still got his come in your mouth, haven't you? You let that fat old pig come in your mouth, didn't you?" I pulled my finger out and slapped him across the mouth.

I don't think anybody had ever done anything like that to him before. He looked up at me and his eyes glazed over with excitement. His hands were suddenly all over my crotch, groping and squeezing. I slapped them away.

"Pig." I raised my hand to his mouth again and stuffed my

middle finger inside. He choked at first, then I felt the back of his throat undulating against my fingertip as he started to swallow and suck. He had a talent for it, no doubt about it.

"That's it. Yeah. You'll suck on anything, won't you? How many guys you let fuck you in the mouth tonight, huh? You let 'em all come in your mouth? You must have a belly full of it by now. Stupid kid."

I pushed his head way back, skewered another two fingers down his throat, giving him something substantial to suck on. Ran the fingers of my other hand down his bulging neck and squeezed, feeling the bulk in his throat. "Damn loose, kid. All those other guys screwing your throat, got it all stretched out. I don't know if I can get a decent fuck out of that or not."

I let him go and stepped back. He reached for my crotch again. I knocked his hand away. "Take off your clothes."

By the weird flickering light of the little video screen, Jonah stripped for me. There wasn't much to take off—ratty T-shirt, faded jeans, white cotton briefs. He stood up straight, hands at his sides, his hard lean chest rising and falling in shallow, agitated breaths. I tweaked his nipples, made him flinch. Ran my hands over his flat belly and narrow hips, took his sturdy little erection in my fist. I gave it a hard squeeze, pulling a gasp out of him, then bent his cock down and released it, letting it slap up against his belly with a sharp, meaty crack.

"Get dressed." I opened the door. "I'll be waiting on the sidewalk outside."

For a second I held the door wide open, with Jonah standing there stark naked and erect, letting the cruisers outside get a quick glance before I slammed it shut on his startled face.

That was how it started. With Jonah following me home, walking along beside me, casting furtive glances down at the

straining seam of my fly. After all the cocks he'd sucked in the
bookstore, he was still hungry for more.

We passed an all-night doughnut shop on the way. I turned
to him and smiled. "Hungry, kid?"

I meant it as a joke, but he took it literally. "No," he said,
with an impatient little shake of his head and another hard look
at my basket.

"But I wanna get some coffee. Come on."

The place was deserted except for a few derelicts and a table
of rowdy frat boys at the back. I ordered a cup of coffee from
the tired-looking waitress, and for Jonah, a long, thick éclair
stuffed with cream.

"But I told you I'm not hungry," he pouted.

"Open your mouth."

That was an order he could understand. He parted his lips
and flattened his tongue—automatically, without question.
Jonah was the original boy who couldn't say no. Self-trained
to suck on cue. While the derelicts snoozed and the waitress
raised her painted eyebrows, and the frat boys giggled and
muttered *faggot* and *queer,* I slowly fed the éclair into Jonah's
waiting, open mouth—playing with him, making him keep
it open while I stuffed it in and then withdrew it an inch or
two, smearing his lips with a sweet white glaze, watching his
Adam's apple bob and his face blush flaming red, watching the
saliva leak from the corners of his straining mouth and trickle
down his chin.

I stuffed the last of it down his throat. He swallowed hard,
wiped his mouth and gave me a look of pure hatred. The frat
boys were staring at him, sniggering in low drunken voices.
From the look on his face I thought he might start crying.

"Come on," I said. "I got something better to feed you at my
place."

I got up and pitched a quarter on the counter, turned and headed for the door. Jonah stayed where he was, glaring at me. I hit the sidewalk and started walking, fast, not waiting for him.

I reached the end of the block and rounded a corner, wondering if I had lost him but refusing to look back. I just kept walking. Then I heard the sound of hard breathing and tennis shoes slapping the sidewalk behind me, and smiled. Jonah was running to catch up.

Jonah may have had a lot of experience sucking cock, but no one had ever actually *taught* him how to do it. And it's possible— no, probable—that he'd never had a cock as big as mine to practice on. I didn't expect much from him, except enthusiasm.

Sure enough, Jonah's eyes were bigger than his mouth. Jonah gagged. Jonah retched. Jonah impaled his throat on my cock and pulled off with a desperate shudder. He kneeled naked and sweaty at the foot of my bed, frantically masturbating, staring slack-jawed at my cock. The shaft reared up marble stiff from my crotch, slick with spit and mucus dredged from deep in Jonah's throat, arching up and then down, the head grazing a cluster of muscles a few inches above my navel.

Jonah—wanting it, grabbing it, trying again. He would squeal when I'd box his ear and hiss at him for using his teeth. Like a dog worrying a bone, Jonah wouldn't give up. He always came back for more.

At some point I grabbed the scruff of his neck and pulled him off, watching his lips glide up the length of my cock and slide over the flaring head with a pop. He stared up at me drunkenly, a trail of milky saliva oozing from his lips and falling onto the sweat-damp sheets.

"Maybe it's time we were properly introduced," I said. "Unless you just want me to call you Dick-hound." His cock gave a sudden twitch, bobbing up and down. He liked that kind of talk.

"Jonah," he said—and then released a long rasping belch, an involuntary burp, the penalty for swallowing too fast. He lowered his eyes and blushed. I grabbed my cock at the base and rubbed it against his downy red cheeks. He narrowed his eyes and opened his mouth, at first in a sigh, then wider, hungry to be fed again. It was like a mechanical reaction—the proximity of a cock near his lips automatically driving the hinge of his jaw straight down.

I ran the moist, blunt tip of my cock over his lips, silk against satin. I looked down, comparing the thickness of the shaft and the smallness of his mouth, wondering how it could ever fit. "Jonah," I crooned. "Jonah and the whale. Only this time, it's the boy who's gonna swallow the whale."

I grabbed his hips and swung him around on his side so that his crotch was in front of my face. I heard him gasp, felt his tongue caress my cock. Maybe he thought I was planning on sucking him in return.

I reached over his hips to the bedside table and brought back a narrow cock-strap, five inches of leather fitted with snaps. One size fits all. On myself I use the outermost snaps, maximum circumference. For Jonah I used the smallest setting, drawing the strap tight around the base of his genitals and snapping it shut. He flinched and squirmed, making a muffled noise around my dick.

I reached toward the table again, for a bottle of lube. I drew back from his crotch, at the same time grinding my hips into his face and my cock deeper down his throat. The tight strap gave his cock a hard, bloated look and pushed his balls upward like a knotted pouch, red and shiny as an apple. I greased him up, dabbing my fingers with oil, running my fingertips over the taut, swollen flesh of his genitals, making the satiny skin glisten and shine. Gently squeezing and thumping his balls, running my fingertips down the underside of his cock, watching it twitch. Jonah responded—moaning, whimpering, deep-throating me while I played with his hard dick.

I'm always surprised by the hypersensitivity of a small cock— as if all the nerve endings were packed closer together, making the whole shaft almost unbearably responsive and tender. Barely touching him, I brought him close within seconds. I toyed with the effect, stroking him lightly between my forefinger and thumb, feeling him tighten and moan around my cock— then releasing him, giving his shaft a little slap and his balls a squeeze, grinding my cock down his throat. Bringing him to the verge of shooting over and over, then pulling back.

For a while I let him suck me at his own pace, working the tight ring of his lips up and down the length of my cock, nursing like a baby on a bottle—until I was ready to face-fuck him. I pulled his hands off my hips, crossed his wrists behind his back and held them in place with one hand. Spread my fingers over the back of his head, like palming a basketball, and pushed it into my crotch. I slid my cock all the way down his throat until my balls were scrubbing his chin.

I like to fuck hard. His throat could take it. I listened to the gagging sounds rising up from deep in his neck, felt the vibrations rippling through my dick. Saliva spewed out of his mouth, all over my cock, like oil lubricating a driving piston. His whole face was slick with spit. I could hear my balls slapping against his forehead.

Jonah's dick stayed rock hard, plump and swollen from the strap. So close I could make him whimper on the verge of coming just by running my fingertip down the shaft. I cradled his balls in the palm of my hand and pulled them sharply back between his legs, making his hard-on stand straight out, raking my fingernails over it, pinching the tip, slapping it back and forth while I screwed his throat. His dick craved it. Hard-ons don't lie. Every time I spanked his cock it snapped straight up again, ready and eager for the next hard slap.

I made him shoot that way—writhing and grunting louder and louder, sending a humming vibration through my cock while I kept up a steady rhythm of hard stinging slaps to his dick, slapping till his cock was red and swollen and aching. One more slap—and then it suddenly grew another inch and started spitting. I pulled my hand away and watched him come without being touched, his cock jerking and spilling itself into empty space while I drew out of his throat and shot my load all over his face.

Afterward, Jonah went all shy and self-conscious on me, turning his face away, pulling himself from the bed, reaching for his clothes. Muttering, "I really gotta go," and wiping the slag from his cheeks with a gesture of self-disgust.

Sometimes the really wild boys are like that—sexual Jekyll-and-Hydes, demons from hell until the moment they come, after which they turn into shamefaced choirboys. I went along with the game, but I didn't let him get away with it. Instead I reached toward the bedside table again, opening the box of condoms I keep there. I rather enjoyed the fantasy of overpowering an innocent choirboy, spanking and deflowering his virgin ass against his squealing protests. So did Jonah. Hard-ons don't lie.

Jonah never goes to the bookstore anymore. He tells me there's only one man he's interested in now. I tell him that's for the best. A guy like Jonah, hungry all the time and half nuts with hormones, needs an incentive to keep him off the streets. He needs a focus for all that hunger. He needs a big cock waiting for him whenever the urge strikes, standing up thick and hard and ready to satisfy his craving. I'm happy to oblige, any time.

As a matter of fact, at this very moment, sitting here at midnight at the keyboard, typing out our story, I'm beginning to feel a familiar sensation between my legs. Smooth cheeks with just a trace of stubble, blushing-warm against the insides of my thighs. A mass of soft, thick curls brushing my stomach. A warm, clutching heat swallowing me dick-first, drawing the blood downward from my brain, making it difficult to concentrate on the next sentence, making it impossible to write even one more...

FRANCOIS AT THE *TOILETTE*

Gerard Wozek

I know he'll be here. Every Thursday afternoon at four, for the past three weeks, I have come to this Métro latrine in the Gare de l'Est station to meet my new lover, Francois.

It's always the same routine. I arrive to greet his uncut cock standing straight up at the urinal. I take my own out and begin to gently stroke my lengthening shaft. Then we move quietly to a stall to finish off our compulsion for each other's skin: the soft biting and gentle nibbles of earlobes and lips, and our fetish for sucking each other's dirty fingers that have been riding steadily up our asses.

After four months of living in Paris, I have yet to visit the *Mona Lisa* at the Louvre or make a pilgrimage to the top of the Eiffel Tower. But I know the section in Père Lachaise Cemetery where half-clothed men linger in mausoleums to get quickie blow jobs. I know the promenade of horny strangers in the Tuileries Garden, just like the back of my Plan du Paris. I'm all too acquainted with the cruisy park at the east of the Ile St.

Louis by the Seine, where you can kiss another guy amid the festive colored lights of the Bateau Mouche. I even know the little bridge at the Rue de la Mare where you can hook a trick in a matter of minutes, even when it's raining.

But it's Francois I breathe for now. His soft brown eyes and full lips framed by a well-trimmed goatee. The tufts of brown chest hair that curl out from over the top of his thick Shetland wool sweaters. The tiny blue star tattooed on his wrist that moves gently over his hanging balls.

At exactly four o'clock, I hand my *centimes* over to the white-haired attendant sitting at a little booth. She is fumbling with a cassette of old Jane Birkin tunes. She snaps the antique plastic into a small player and when the slow music begins I become invisible to her. The turnstile cranks and I walk up to a row of men, mostly middle-aged mustaches, all standing with their zippers down at the latrine. Their eyes scrape my painted leather jacket, the flag patch on my worn jeans, my Marine crew cut.

"*Allemagne*," someone whispers and leers toward my direction, my soft dick barely out past the edge of my buttonhole crotch.

I move toward the stalls in the back of the latrine, but there is a herd waiting to get inside an empty one. So I stand with my hand on my cock at the urinal, covering my rising shaft, while everyone becomes somewhat agitated. There are craning necks and mutual hand jobs resuming all around me, but I remain focused on Francois.

He has just arrived and stepped up to the row of jerking Frenchmen. His foreskin is the color of burnt copper. Around his swelling shaft is a yellow suede cock ring with spindly metal studs. The acrid smell of amyl nitrate emanates from the other side of the latrine and meshes with the odor of stale piss and cum. I watch my cohort as his nostrils flare and we both begin to grin.

"I hoped you would come." His accent is thick and for a moment drowns out the chanteuse on the tinny boom box.

"I haven't come yet, but I'm planning on it." I whisper delicately across the corroded urinals. "*Mon cher.*"

His eyes roll back for a moment as he rolls the tip of his thumb across the giant head of his uncut cock. I can smell the sweat and stale urine at the tip and I feel my knees beginning to give. The crowd has finally dispersed from around the toilets and I follow him into an open pen. The scarred metal door closes behind us and I watch as he drops his dark corduroy trousers and sits down on the toilet seat.

I have quickly straddled myself over his dark, hairless legs. His lips are thick and rough and the color of freshly iced salmon. He wears a knotted kerchief around his neck, which smells like lemony vervain, and he takes it off and wraps it around the back of my head and pulls me up to his wet tongue as though his parted mouth were an oxygen mask. Breathing him in, I can almost forget that I am in a dank toilet near the Métro.

The mournful chords of "*Ne Me Quitte Pas*" float over the stench and our rhythmic jostle. Jane Birkin keeps mixing in American words with her French and as Francois begins to thrust, I can't help but focus on an open page in his open art journal. I spy a page of tightly knit cursive French words and tornado scribbles surrounding the elegant swirls of a trained artist's hand: profiles of young men, the curves of an ancient streetlamp, then, a perfectly drawn angel, something you would see pestering a nativity scene or the mantle of cathedral altar, writhing in ecstatic terror. The body is placid but the head is askew, the mouth agape as though a horrific scream were passing through it.

I am bouncing on the legs of my lover. I am reaching for a coat hook to balance myself. The turnstile is cranking and Jane Birkin begins to sound more and more like Marlene Dietrich. If I close my eyes I can imagine a cabaret, just like the one in *Blonde Venus,* and there are swooning legionaries and a stream of smoke from my clove cigarette billowing through my nostrils and I am the vision of love, just like the key-lit icon, in a sequined gown with blue star earrings in the shape of Francois's tattoo. No one can take his eyes off my neon skin, my smoky eyes, the perfect points of my fingernails. I keep my eyes tightly shut, my lover keeps thrusting and the film just keeps rolling on.

In one scene I'm Ingrid Bergman in the movie *Casablanca,* spilling champagne glasses across a café table and clutching the shoulder of Humphrey Bogart. In the next frame, I'm Gene Kelly in a tight striped T-shirt, whirling under the sanitized bridges near the Seine. With my eyes closed, I can see the invented Paris of my childhood, the Paris fed by Saturday afternoon musicals, generic encyclopedia articles and assorted travel guides stowed away in my suitcase.

In my mind I move aboveground. I read Colette in French in the Luxembourg Gardens. I wipe Nutella off my lover's chin at the Place Vendôme. I write postcards to the friends I've left behind, extolling the views of the Seine from the Pont Alexandre. In my head, I live in Paris—the city that breathes and exists somewhere out beyond this rancid train station piss palace.

But where I open my eyes, that urban wander ground vanishes. Francois licks cooling *riz au lait* off my chest hair and lets his tongue wander down from my musky armpit to my quivering pelvis. He sips on a chilled Orangina then resumes his gentle nose nudge down to my groin and balls. Eyes peer through screw holes pierced through the sides of the stall as my French lover opens a second condom, preparing to make another entry into my anxiously poised body.

"You may enter, *monsieur.*"

He rides me, softly at first, then we both crank our way into a syncopated crescendo. In the space between ecstasy and wiping the spilled seed from our rolled-down pants and the concrete floor, I attempt to secure another rendezvous by exchanging phone numbers. As he pulls his sticky sweater over his head, I motion with my hand as though writing with a pen, "Number... telephone?"

Francois shrugs with a soft roll of his eyes, opens the stall door and with a tilt of his head, exits the *toilette.*

With a determined charge in my pulse, I buckle my jeans and make off toward the Métro, where I can see that my estranged lover has bolted through the gate toward the destination point, La Courneuve. I pass my ticket through the entrance and keep several paces behind Francois. When the crowded subway pulls in, I jump on the car behind and keep my head turned toward the glass car doors so I can view him

Chateau Landon. Stalingrad. Riquet. The train stops at each Métro station, and still he doesn't leave his seat. I'm imagining the pulsing world aboveground. I'm imagining the tourists taking snapshots of the sun going down behind the Conciergerie, or the last hints of twilight off the glass pyramid entrance to the Louvre, the children taking their boats out of the fountain at the Luxembourg Gardens, or the gray stones mute against the flashing neon of the Champs Elysees. Crimee. Corentin Cariou. I'm riveted to his body and still he doesn't move.

Porte de la Villette. Finally he moves toward the door. I step off the car then follow him down a narrow artery. There are drunken beggars singing some strangely familiar American pop tune and the faint smell of cherry-infused tobacco from the trail

of Francois's lit cigarette tip. I wend up stairs and more narrow
tubular passageways. Again, I'm paces behind him and shad-
owed behind the heft of a backpacker's overstuffed sack.

How do you make love to someone as though you were
traversing a great city? How do you fornicate without inhibition
as though you were encountering the foreign smells of an urban
market for the first time? I can think only of my lover's gentle
thrusting, his thick lips on my eyelids, the smell of his sweet
breath, the long trail of sweat running from his temples down
his neck. I think of his insatiable kisses, the sucking of his heavy
lower lip, the electric pulse that seems to run through us, the
humming connecting current, as I take all of him inside of me.

Finally, we reach the upper terminal. Francois pauses to rub
out his cigarette with the tip of his brown boot. He tosses some
euros into a vending machine that dispenses a small tin of some
sort of candy, then enters what appears to be another latrine.

I stand outside the *toilette,* brooding over whether or not
to enter. My groin is still on fire from the stubble of his beard
against my own chafed foreskin. I pass some coins onto the
matron's plate and enter the white-tiled public restroom. There
are three stalls. Two of them with closed doors. I gingerly enter
the unoccupied one and situate myself upon the porcelain bowl.

Peering through a wide bolt hole the size of a quarter, I begin
to recognize Francois's unshaven chin in the next stall. His full
lips are moving up and around another man's firm buttocks. I
watch as he pushes open the dark hairy asscrack with his fingers
and begins to pleasure the man's hole with his extended tongue.
A deep sigh permeates the warm enclosure next to me and Francois's cohort begins to bend over more completely.

I open the buttons of my fly and my hardening cock pops out. I
am the voyeur now, the blinking eye at the stained peephole, the
stroking onlooker. I can hear indecipherable words, moaning, a

guttural laughter. Francois tears open a condom and begins to wrap on his second skin. Then I take it all in: the slow mount, the straddle around the toilet bowl, the athletic thrusting and pumping, torso to torso. I peer up to see the animal-like flaring of Francois's nostrils. I imagine his breath again, his slow drool dripping down my own neck, and in a matter of minutes, the three of us collapse into a storm of moans.

I try to swallow my gasps. There is a sudden silence that takes over the latrine. I listen for the untangling of dropped trousers and belts. The wiping of sweat from brows with toilet paper. The awkward shuffling apart.

I slowly open the stall door and watch the dark stranger emerge: a Moroccan gentleman I think for a moment, though I'm not entirely sure. Then Francois steps out, emerging like a Napoleonic swordsman, a stealthy warrior after meeting the challenge of his quest.

I somehow find the core within me to call out, "Francois, *mon cher.*"

He turns for a moment, as though startled by the shrill echo reverberating through the stark bathroom. In the fluorescent light, his skin looks somewhat sallow, his sunken eyes less familiar, world-weary, irretrievably jaded even.

I'm still gushing, "Francois, *mon ami.*" I know there are still pearls of drying cum on my hand as I extend it toward his frozen stance. "*Sil vous plait.*"

I suddenly recall a moment in Jean Luc Godard's classic film, *Pierrot Le Fou,* where the protagonist looks back for a moment at the fading background of Paris. It all seems to be washing away, crumpling in torn shreds behind his stony face. I stand, momentarily unable to move, as I watch Francois make his way toward the exit.

I quickly gather my things up and run out to see my

Frenchman popping a small lozenge into his mouth as he hastily turns the corner of a narrow walkway.

So this is how the French kiss you good-bye, I think.

I wipe the last remains of my secret lover from off my mouth. From the corner of my eye I spot a giant poster advertising a McDonald's Happy Meal. I stand there staring at a giant-sized mouth that seems ready to devour both a hamburger and my bewildered face. I close my eyes in order to escape this scene, but the discombobulating storyline continues.

I head back toward the Métro ticket station, but I don't return to the subway. I walk up the stairs where my imagined city has been waiting patiently for me, like a distant lover, like an estranged companion.

I emerge from the stairwell into a colorless neighborhood in the nineteenth arrondissement. I gaze around, still disoriented, and approach a small fenced-in park situated next to a low-budget brasserie with two small tables set out in front.

It isn't the Paris of old movie stars or even the one I fabricated in my childhood. But it's the stop I got off at.

There are mustache men casually leaning on a railing, some who almost resemble the profiles of the guys caricatured in Francois's art journal. One of them draws me in with an almost half smile, an almost sneer.

"*Bonsoir,*" the chap whispers under his breath to catch the rim of my passing silver earring.

I turn around for a moment to make contact and he's looking beyond me, gaping at some exquisite French boy emerging from the Métro stairwell. So I continue on toward the edge of the nearest street corner and far in the distance, if I stand on my toes a bit, I can almost manage to see what appears to be the top of the Eiffel Tower.

I finally take in a deep breath and the sooty exhaust fumes

aboveground here suit me just fine. I dislodge my Plan du Paris from my shoulder bag, and go toward something else, maybe it's Paris, maybe it's just a myth in my head, but it continues to linger in the air like a ponderous, unanswered question.

MUSCLE ARCADE

Bearmuffin

All the hunks were at the mall yesterday when I decided to go buy a new jockstrap. I almost got whiplash looking at this one and that as they passed me by. Until I spotted the hottest stud of them all, Steve Preston.

Steve was our star quarterback and he was standing in front of the adult bookstore gazing at a display of long, thick dildos. The store was notorious because everyone on campus knew the hottest jocks went there to get their cocks sucked.

A powerful jawline, sharp nose, sensuous full lips, and blond wavy locks sweeping down over his thick bull-neck completed the picture of your classic All-American jock stud.

Steve's hefty muscles bulged under his college varsity football team jacket. The dude had a firm bubble-butt packed in tight jeans. Just one glance at Steve's magnificent ass and I fell in lust. I couldn't resist this tempting vision of masculine beauty. When he went inside the store, I had to follow him.

I couldn't find him at first. Fuck! Had he disappeared into a cubicle? Had someone already wrapped his anxious lips around a cock that by rights was mine? No! Luckily, I spotted him at the magazine rack flipping through *Jock Lust*.

I stood behind Steve as he carefully studied a photo of a humpy dude getting a blow job. Steve sighed loudly as his hand flew down toward his cock. His thick meat swelled lustfully, snaking temptingly down his thigh.

I blurted out impulsively, "That stud has nothing on you!" Steve dropped the magazine and turned around. The dude was red-faced with embarrassment just because I'd caught him checking out a gay magazine. Yeah, he was straight all right, but curious, too.

"Hey, dude," I said soothingly. "It's no biggie. It's cool to check out other dudes. Doesn't mean you're a homo."

I picked up the magazine and put it back on the stand. "Work out a lot?" My question elicited a shit-eating grin from Steve. He squeezed his crotch. "Yeah," he said proudly.

I just grinned back at him. "You queer?" he asked in a hoarse whisper. I noticed that his eyes were sparkling with interest.

"Sure fuckin' is," I replied. My horny grin matched his leering smile.

"Fuck, dude! I'm so fucking horny I could fuck a horse!" Steve hissed as he rubbed his cock struggling underneath the faded denim. A precum stain suddenly appeared right at the head which was poking out obscenely like a beer can.

I licked my lips. "C'mere," I said, grabbing my own crank. "I know how to take care of that!" I was acting as cool as I could but my heart was leaping in my throat. Fuck! I was about to blow a fucking two-hundred-pound six-foot-two jock virgin!

"Just follow me!" I said.

I made my way down the row of cubicles until I reached the last one. I crept inside, leaving the door ajar. The seconds seemed

like hours as I waited for Steve to appear. Finally, I heard his big
feet padding on the linoleum. Steve cautiously opened the door
and looked in. Then he sneaked inside, locking the door behind
him.

I put a token into the coin box and a porn movie began flickering on the wall. Steve's heavy breathing and masculine odor
were arousing me. I saw a trickle of sweat cascade down his
temple. He was nervous as hell.

"Your first time?" I asked. He nodded. "Relax dude," I said.
"It's cool!" I boldly took hold of his jacket and slowly slipped it
off him, letting it fall to the floor. "Fuck!" I gasped as my eyes
took in his powerful physique crowned by his dazzling upper
torso. "You're a beauty!"

The dude was just plain fuckin' huge! Steve's nipples were
thick and erect, jutting boldly against his white T-shirt, which
was stretched taut over his super pecs and thrilling abdominals.
His thick arms splayed away from his rib cage. His shoulders
were massively corded. My jaw hit the floor. "What a fuckin'
hot bod!" I exclaimed.

Steve smiled at my compliment and stepped closer to me. I
could feel his throbbing crotch slowly grinding against mine.
The dude was beginning to relax so I put my hands over his
brawny chest and began massaging it. His chest muscles felt like
steel plates underneath my sweaty palms.

"Mmm," Steve sighed. "Feels good."

"This'll feel even better," I said. I pulled him closer to me
and nuzzled my head between his head and shoulder. I ran my
tongue all over his thick neck while I savored the manly taste
of his pungent sweat. Steve's strong masculine odor was heady,
arousing me so that my cock just about leaped out of my shorts.

Steve must have felt my cock throb against his own because
I soon felt his fingers move down to my crotch and squeeze. My

zipper rasped as Steve slowly pulled it down. I grabbed Steve and began kissing him. My lips eagerly pressed against Steve's feverish mouth as his fingers slipped past my briefs' pee-flap and rubbed over my aching cock.

Steve dipped his tongue into my mouth and I sighed with ecstasy while his fingers strummed on my turgid shaft. I was so caught up with his wild kiss: our tongues mashed together, our lips joined as one. He jacked me off until I felt a wild rumbling in my balls.

"You've got a big cock," Steve sighed.

"Bet it's not as big as yours," I countered, pulling away from him for a moment to catch my breath.

I quickly sank to my knees and rubbed my face against his groin, enjoying the sensation of his cock throbbing lustfully against his fly. Then I took hold of his belt buckle and unloosened it and slowly unbuttoned his jeans.

Just as I undid the last button, his cock surged forth, straining lewdly against the crotch of his briefs, writhing unashamedly underneath the white cotton.

My eyes were glued to the bulbous head prodding through the pee-flap as I quickly yanked down his jeans over his brawny thighs. I watched his cock shoot through the pee-flap until five mouth-watering inches of prime grade-A stud cock was in full view.

I marveled at the size of Steve's veins crisscrossing the immense ivory-pinkish shaft. My lips trembled when I saw a luscious drop of precum glistening invitingly at the very tip of the shaft. My tongue snaked out to lap up the drop. I heartily enjoyed the ripe flavor of his potent jizz. I couldn't wait for him to shoot a huge thrilling load down my hungry throat.

"Suck my balls," I heard Steve gasp as his hands glided through my hair. I pulled down his briefs and his cock snapped up against his taut belly. I took a moment to lick around his belly button, tracing down over the hairy trail that led down to his musky groin where I inhaled deeply of his powerful masculine fragrance before finally landing my tongue on his low-danglers.

Steve's balls were smooth. I gingerly licked over them until he gasped, "Oh, god!" and I felt him tugging at my hair again. I laved one nut and then the other and then opened my mouth as both testicles descended past my lips. I hummed merrily until he was sighing with ecstasy. "Oh, fuck," he gasped. "Blow me dude! Blow me!!!"

Steve's erection was bobbing before my very eyes. I gasped at his mighty meat for a moment before leaning forward to take his rock-hard cock into my mouth. Steve moaned and whimpered as my lips suctioned hard around his pulsing shaft until I had elicited wild, lusty grunts that shot from the back of his throat.

"Awww fuck!" Steve yelled. I slowly suctioned backward, letting his cock momentarily slip from my sweaty lips before reapplying my tongue along the shaft, gently lapping against his throbbing veins, dipping into the piss slit and then circling around and underneath the shaft.

"Fuck!!!" Steve bellowed.

I took his nuts into my mouth, swallowed his meat to the base.

"Open wide, dude!" he grunted. His beautiful eyes sparkled; his mouth was twisted with a lustful snarl. "I wanna face-fuck you!"

Steve thrust his hips, sliding his cock into my mouth. He pulled and tugged on his own tits as his cock hurtled down my gag-wrenched throat. I knew he was about to come with all his moaning and groaning. Yeah, the dude had a big load.

"I want you to take it, good buddy!" Steve gasped. "Yeah!" I opened my throat as wide as I could and hunkered down on his cock until the head crashed against my tonsils, all the way down until my nose was buried in his musky pubes.

"Aww yeah, fuck, yeah!" Steve screamed as I grabbed his balls and yanked on them. Steve pushed forward and emptied his load right into my mouth.

I'd swallowed plenty of loads but none this sweet—so tangy with just a bit of musk. Steve's hands roamed over my head, pressing down hard, as he mashed his groin against my face. His cock surged and swelled inside my mouth like a fire hose gone out of control as he emptied spurts and spurts of raging jock jizz over my tongue.

I swallowed as much as I could, but the rest just spurted out and splashed on my face and chest. Even when I pulled my mouth off, I still got a few heavy cum-spurts right in the kisser as Steve's cock kept on shooting its heavy load.

Finally, I licked the last cum-drop from the corner of my mouth.

"Thanks, bud," Steve whispered, buttoning his fly. "You gonna be here tomorrow?"

"Fuckin' A I will," I replied with a grin.

"Me, too," he hissed. "And this time I'll blow you!"

My cocksucking prowess had turned a first timer into a regular customer.

THE WALL FETISH

Bob Masters

Tommy Russo looked at himself in the mirror attached to the concrete wall of his small dorm. The pale, whitish glow emanating from the fluorescent lighting fixture above it cast his features in an otherworldly haze. Still, he thought to himself, he didn't look too bad. Twenty years old and filling out in all the best ways. Gone was the youthful gangliness that had made him feel awkward and self-conscious since he was sixteen. Now he had a solid chest and bulging arms. His abs were firm and tight and his legs felt like iron. Hours spent in the gym were finally paying off.

Tommy brushed his thick black hair away from his eyes and tried to shift his consciousness into an objective appraisal of how good looking he really was. His naturally dark, olive-toned skin and jet-black hair made his Italian heritage obvious. His features were beginning to settle into that half-boyish, half-mannish appearance that most twenty-year-old boys had. He was better than average looking. Maybe it was his large, brown eyes, hooded as they were by heavy lids with long, black lashes. He took a deep breath and reached for his backpack before heading for the door of his dorm room. Tommy felt like he was becoming a man. He liked the lithe grace that his muscles afforded him. He also liked the sense of freedom that his first year away from home was giving him. His first two years in his hometown community college had saved his parents a lot of money. But he had grown restless. Now he was set free. He could come and go as he pleased. His roommate was okay, a little—no, make that a lot—more sophisticated than he was. Charlie was from Chicago and never tired of pointing out how small Tommy's hometown was in comparison. Tommy had to act a little dumbfounded now and then just to make Charlie feel justified in his big-city superiority. Tommy knew he came from a glorified farm town with one or two industries and had a lot to learn. He didn't mind. Every day was a mind-blowing experience as far as he was concerned. He wasn't about to let on just how different and better life on the big campus was for him compared to the rural and insular town he had been raised in. So he took his roommate's ribbing with a grain of salt. Besides, he could tell that, deep down, Charlie was just as unsure as he was. The long discussions they had shared late at night had shown him that a large part of Charlie's bragging was just a front. Charlie also wondered and worried about the future, about his grades, about his appearance. He had even complimented Tommy on his muscular physique once, couching it in a semi-sarcastic remark about "farm diets," of course, but Tommy could tell he meant it.

It has to be an awkward time for everyone, Tommy thought as he made his way across the crowded campus quad toward the library. *We are not quite boys and not quite men.* And then there was the big issue, sex. Charlie had pestered and pestered him to talk about his sex life, bragging how he had bagged girl after girl in the big city of Chicago. But for all that he could tell, Charlie had never once brought any girl back to the dorm room and was just as single as he was. That made it easier for Tommy to evade his questions. He was not about to tell Charlie that he was still a virgin. That his parents were old-fashioned about dating. That he had himself been physically awkward and shy all through his teenage years. It wasn't really until he had arrived here that he felt a growing confidence that he was attractive and desirable.

But that hadn't led to any dates or girlfriends. Tommy really didn't feel any urgency to get involved in any complication that might compromise the sense of freedom he was reveling in. Sex was the farthest thing from his mind, really, as he bounded up the steps of the library and entered the fourth-floor library restroom. No, sex was not a preoccupation as he swung open a stall door in the row of toilets in the dimly lit atmosphere and proceeded to unbuckle his belt. He felt relaxed and somewhat absentminded as he pulled his slacks down his muscular legs together with his underwear. He sat down, the cool plastic seat cover meeting his flexing muscular butt impartially. The silence and solitude were conducive to relaxation and he soaked in the quiet ambience of the quotidian grotto. His body performed its duty and he let his eyes idly wander over the walls. He was mildly surprised to find a vast scrollwork of graffiti extending from top to bottom. It was of every size, shape and color. Evidently young male students liked to express themselves while they answered the call of nature. He read a few of the pithy witticisms that only college minds can think of before his attention was suddenly arrested by the centerpiece situated higher up in the middle of the wall to his right.

It was an expert rendition of a throbbing twelve-inch cock

shooting sperm four feet across the bathroom stall wall. The artist had used a black-inked pen and had taken time to etch the penis in bold black lines. He had even filled in mounds of wiry pubic hair that sprouted from the huge thing's root. The hair cascaded in a tangle of curlicues drawn with a lusty flourish. They extended almost half a foot down, covering a pair of swollen nuts that hung like bowling balls beneath. Great spurts of semen shot out of the shaft like an erupting geyser that stretched to the cubicle door. The drawing was lusty, pornographic and obscene. Tommy couldn't take his eyes off it. He felt his breath quicken and tightness grow in his chest. His heart was pounding. It was all so forbidden. He had never seen anything like it before. He felt his own cock beginning to stir as if in some sympathetic magical response to a primitive totem to male virility. Blood rushed to the space between his legs while adrenaline pulsed through his body. He felt dizzy and light-headed. Tommy ran his eyes up and down the fetishistic image, soaking up its provocative fascination, until his gaze became fixed on a set of scrawled words that had been scratched on the wall underneath the spurting member in the same bold, black ink. They read: *Blow job. 6th Floor Restroom, last stall on the left. After 4 pm.*

That was too much. It drew him up short. He couldn't keep doing this; the intensity was clouding his judgment. He was losing the sense of freedom that had accompanied him all through the morning. He felt confused and apprehensive. Why was he so hot and bothered by a drawing of a huge cock? Surely it was just a case of thrills at seeing someone flaunt the rules so flagrantly. He hadn't realized people could be so bold. Nobody in his hometown would ever have thought of doing something like that. He willed his bulging cock back into his underwear as he stood up. He drew his pants up around his waist and left the cubicle. Standing before the washbasin, he ran cold water over his hands and face, trying to get his composure back. He had to will all of that stimulation away, get back to his schoolwork. He had to do research on the sonnets of Shakespeare. It was almost funny, the sheer contrast of the artist's prank and the dryness of having to sit and read poetry.

Tommy Russo left the restroom and succeeded in keeping his cock tame and flaccid while he plowed through Shakespeare. There was going to be a quiz in his English class at two o'clock this afternoon, so his knowledge of Shakespeare had to be pretty thorough. He tried to concentrate and found that the fourth-floor restroom was like some shining presence that he couldn't shake his awareness from as long as he stayed on that floor. So he decided to go up one floor. He knew it was kind of foolish, that no one looked at him differently after he left the restroom. But he felt different, somehow. He sat and opened the book of poems and realized that his prior life in his parents' home and small town had set him up to feel the fear and apprehension that he had felt. It was just a dirty picture in a public restroom. There were thousands of young people on this campus. Any one of them could have drawn that picture. The large foyer of the fifth-floor study area was a sea of tables that were situated directly across from the fifth-floor restrooms. Tommy sat with his Shakespeare and studied, but he found his eyes looking up every now and then at the boys who entered the restroom some thirty feet away. He found himself sizing them up, looking at the way they walked, how tight their pants were, how long they stayed in there. Then he would direct his attention back to the sonnets and it was pretty apparent that they were love poems written by Shakespeare to another man.

Tommy couldn't help but chuckle at himself, at his back-woods naiveté that was becoming as apparent to him as he read the lines that Shakespeare had penned. Shakespeare wouldn't mind that he had sprouted a hard-on in the public toilet that day. Men probably had sex with men all the time, all through history. No one was the worse for it. The faint sound of the restroom door swinging open made him look up from his text just as a large football player–type strode out. The big man's muscles rippled with each masculine step. He looked so confident and sure of himself, the very picture of macho manhood. Tommy suddenly began to feel certain that he was overestimating how many men had sex with men, that most men were straight and played football or joined the marines....till he noticed that the big guy's eyes had locked on to his. Damn, the guy winked at him! Then he turned and walked down the hallway. Tommy watched the young man's rippling physique and felt his cock grow hard.

This time he decided to let himself enjoy the sensation of desire that flooded his being like a fire rushing out of control. He stared off into the distance for a few seconds, reveling in the vitality of his body's reaction, the rock-hard erection pulsing in his pants. He wondered what the man who inspired Shakespeare had looked like. Was he like that guy who just winked? Was he like Charlie, smooth and wiry? Whatever the object of desire in these poems had looked like, Tommy could feel the intensity of the writer's imagery that so strained at the boundaries of language in order to constrain the fires of lust that lurked just beneath them. Obviously, Shakespeare had found it necessary to hide the physical part of his love for the "gentleman" of his sonnet pieces. Society was probably too rigid and backward to allow man-to-man sexual attraction back then. How much of Tommy's earlier life had been just like that, how much had he absorbed into himself so that he never even allowed himself to feel things like desire for other men? For some reason, the lines of the poem began to pound away at his resistance to accepting that maybe there were aspects of himself that he had kept walled off for too long. Only now were the pieces falling into place, like a huge jigsaw puzzle that was slowly taking shape. The picture that was emerging was intoxicating and intense, the words to describe it still indistinct and unformed. But the words of the sonnets helped him search for them and they all seemed to echo with the promise of the message scrawled on the toilet-stall wall.

He would go to lunch, go to class, pass his exam, and then work out for an hour. He would pump his muscles until they bulged with pure masculine power. Images of the picture on the fourth-floor stall flashed through his mind. Yes, he would take the necessary action to go one step further. He would take up that anonymous writer's promise that was so wantonly scrawled in indelible ink. It was impossible to erase, not for him.

Tommy felt the hot water cascade over his rippling muscles as he showered off in the locker room showers of the university gym. He had enjoyed an intense workout. He was certain he had aced the exam on Shakespeare. It had been an essay test. He found the words to write the essay poured from him easily, as if he had an understanding that was beyond just intellectual knowledge. The poetry had let him feel things that were sprouting all through him like some wild jungle growth that knew no boundaries. It was a strange exhilaration that spoke of things only men his age could feel, desires and needs that only an inner circle could understand, like a secret brotherhood of lovers. His excitement grew. He felt his immaturity vanish with each passing moment, new insights into his own sexual nature rising to the surface. How could he have lived so long without ever realizing that he needed to feel the touch of a man? Why did the sun seem to burn brighter and the birds to sing louder?

He had all the time in the world to figure that out. Today he was just happy to pump up his pecs and glutes. Somehow, it was those muscles that he wanted to accentuate. It made him feel a little dirty and a little sexy to work out those muscles. He wanted his pecs to bulge and his ass to stick out.

He enjoyed taking the shower too. He imagined the other boys watching him. Who knew if it was really true, but it was fun to picture them doing it, maybe rubbing their crotches as they eyed his young and muscular physique. He subtly flexed his biceps and wiggled his ass as he rubbed the soap over every inch of his naked body. The soapsuds glistened on the hair of his chest and legs and he made a point of working it up into a rich lather that squished and foamed against his hairy Italian skin. He provocatively bent over, spreading his legs apart and flexing his ass muscles so all could see. It was like there was a tiger inside him that needed to run free. He would ride that tiger. Yes, he decided, he would ride that fabulous beast long and hard, and he would begin this afternoon.

Tommy dressed himself in a dreamy, almost languorous state, pausing to feel the fabric fit tight against his chest and ass. He then threw his gym bag back into the locker and fastened the padlock like he was fastening his innocent and stupid past away from him. He strode outside the gymnasium and into the hot autumn sun that felt like cotton candy caressing his tender flesh. The magnet that was the library drew him onward. He did not even pause to consider the abandon with which he made his way toward his rendezvous.

When he reached the steps of the library, his legs carried him forward like he was some automaton. Any chance for fear or second-guessing was banished from his mind. It was as if twenty years of denial were being trodden underfoot. He would not stop to consider that this could not be right or possible. In fact, he even rode the elevator up to the sixth floor, something he usually didn't do, preferring to take the stairs in the interest of keeping in good shape. Only now he knew why he wanted to be in good shape. He wanted to have good sex.

The library was not too crowded at this time of day, at least not on the sixth floor. Tommy strode down the hallway from the elevator doors and headed toward the restroom. He felt his breath give a little as he swung its door open and stepped in. His cock had begun to grow semi-hard in the elevator and now he felt it stiffening ramrod straight and straining against the fabric of his pants. His pulse began to race. But he continued to step forward toward the last stall on the left, that one in the corner. He noticed the door to the cubicle next to it was unlocked, so he pushed it open and stepped in. A hole had been crudely drilled in the wall separating the cubicles. That was interesting. Right now it was urgent that he set his raging cock free from the confines of his pants. It was beginning to hurt. He unbuckled his belt and pulled his pants and underwear down. His erect penis sprung out and bounced against his belly. He seated himself and waited. After a few seconds, he saw fingers emerge through the hole. They wiggled back and forth provocatively. He stood up and leaned over to glance through the hole. A young man, about the same age as him, slender and handsome, was crouching there on his knees. He smiled at Tommy and said in a low voice, "Poke your big cock through the hole and let me suck it, stud."

Tommy thrust his hardened shaft through the hole. He felt the boy's warm tongue work its way up slowly from the base of his cock toward the tip, pausing to lick the edge of his cockhead before slowly working its way down again. Tommy could not believe the sensations that ran through his cock as the boy coaxed and teased his already stiffened penis into even more turgid rigidity. It was pleasure that verged on pain as the young man's tongue worked over his shaft as if worshipping it. Tommy began to feel that he could no longer take the boy's lingering attentions but was shaken from his discomfort as he felt his whole hard cock being swallowed into the cocksucker's greedy mouth. He felt his entire dick plunge deep down the sucking throat. The warm wetness engulfed his throbbing shaft, and Tommy could not help but shudder with the lust that coursed through his trembling frame as the boy swirled his tongue all around his straining, thrusting cock. Tommy settled into the glorious attention being given to his virgin dick and felt like he was actually fucking the fellator's face. Every thrust of his hips made him feel like he was fucking his way to manhood and dominance, emotions of lust and power and strength saturating his mind and body. But when the boy proceeded to bob up and down his cock, slurping and moaning as he pumped the base with his hands, Tommy's attention was nowhere but in the entire length of his throbbing shaft. His hips began to shake uncontrollably, flashes of light cascading through his brain, as gusher after gusher of white-hot cum shot down the cocksucking throat that would not stop its carnal attentions to his spasming shaft. He let out a moan as he felt his liquid essence spurt out from him and enter the gulping mouth on the other side. He collapsed against the stall wall and let his partner cradle his softening dick inside his loving mouth, softly moaning as he swirled his tongue around the softening member. It was if his mouth had been a sexual organ that Tommy had satisfied.

Tommy removed his cock from the hole and sat back on the toilet seat. He needed a minute to catch his breath and consider what he had just experienced. It was one of the most intoxicatingly sensual experiences of his entire life and he could not help but wonder why he had waited until the age of twenty to experience it. He sat for a minute until he caught his breath and then stood and pulled his underwear and pants back up. He buckled his belt and strode through the cubicle door and out into the sixth-floor foyer. It had all been so easy. He walked toward the stairwell and entered, pausing to walk over to the windows and look out over the campus quad. He felt an overwhelming joy inside him. Now he knew what it would take to make him happy. The people below all looked beautiful to him. He could embrace his freedom and love the world. Tommy turned and walked down the steps to the fifth floor.

Once there, he began to walk around the circumference of the floor, pausing to check out the different people he saw sitting at tables or standing among the bookshelves. He had made his way about halfway around before he spied the young man with the football-player build who had winked at him earlier. He was sitting at a table by himself, his nose buried in a physical education textbook. Tommy ducked into a bookshelf aisle and grabbed a book for himself. He nonchalantly strode over and sat directly opposite the young man, opening his book and acting like he was reading. It seemed like he was intent on reading his phys-ed book. But that soon changed. Tommy felt a slight rubbing against his foot, a rubbing that persisted, and he felt a thrill shoot up his legs. He waited until the foot worked its way up to his ankle and seductively grazed against the inside of his leg.

"Hi, I'm Frank," the young man said in a low voice.

"Tommy. Pleased to meet you. Didn't I see you earlier this morning?"

"Sure did. Want to go with me to where you saw me earlier?"

Tommy felt an even greater thrill rush through him. "Sure, that would be great, Frank."

"Let's go!" said Frank. He stood up. Tommy jumped up

and followed him as Frank walked leisurely toward the fifth-floor restroom. Frank held the door open. It was like he had no fear. Tommy followed him as Frank made his way to a stall and motioned for Tommy to follow. Tommy stepped in and Frank shut and locked the door. Then he turned and put his arms around Tommy. The large stud squeezed him and brought his handsome face to Tommy's.

"Let me kiss you," said Frank. Tommy felt the other youth's lips close over his own. The man's powerful tongue entered his mouth and it felt like he was fucking him with it. He pressed Tommy against the cubicle wall, rubbing his body against him while he squeezed his pecs and nipples. Tommy let out a small grunt of surprise. He had never felt anything like that before. Frank broke his kiss and looked at Tommy with a slightly amused expression.

"You like that, baby?" He was breathing heavily and Tommy could not mistake the look of pure desire that was burning there.

"I have never had someone do that to me before. It felt so different. Like my whole body is on fire!"

"Wait till you feel this," said Frank, as he lowered his hands to grasp Tommy's ass. He looked deep into Tommy's eyes and kissed him again while he squeezed his asscheeks and rubbed his crotch against him, thrusting his stiffened dick against Tommy's.

"I want to fuck that sweet ass of yours, muscle-boy. Let Frankie fuck it, huh, baby?" he said as he kissed and licked Tommy's ears and cheeks, rubbing and thrusting his crotch against Tommy in a circular motion while he fondled his ass. Tommy could feel the sheer power of the athletic man's frame as he rocked and pulsed against him. He thrilled at the idea of letting this stud take him, but he wasn't sure if he could do it.

"I have never been fucked before, Frankie. You will have to show me how."

Frankie looked at him with surprise and said, "Don't worry; I'll go easy on you. He pulled a small plastic bottle from his shirt pocket. "This is a lubricating jelly. It will make it easier for you to take me."

Tommy looked at the small plastic bottle and back at Frankie's handsome face. He decided then and there that he would let the huge man fuck him.

"Okay, Frankie, fuck me!"

Frankie unbuckled Tommy's belt and undid his trousers in what seemed like a single motion. Tommy felt his pants pulled down and his body turned around so that he stood facing the cubicle wall. Frankie crouched down behind him and Tommy felt his fingers fasten around the elastic strap on the back of his underpants. Frankie proceeded to pull them down, inch by inch, ever so slowly over his ass while he made *oohing* and *ahing* sounds deep in his throat. It made Tommy feel so hot and attractive to have his butt slowly exposed that way. He couldn't resist flexing his asscheeks for Frankie. He wanted him to drink up the sight of his muscular ass, to admire him. But, when he did, he was shocked. Frankie's tongue thrust up into his ass. Tommy shuddered with sensual surprise as Frankie pressed his tongue into Tommy's asshole, pausing to kiss and smack it with animal desire.

"Oh, my god, Frank; oh, my god. I have never had anyone do that to me before!"

"You just wait, handsome," Frankie said as he stood and undid his own pants. Tommy glanced back and saw the football dude's seven-inch dick standing straight up into the sky as Frankie rubbed it with gobs of lubricant. Frankie's powerful legs were chiseled works of muscular power. He felt Frankie's large hands grasp his waist and then felt the muscleman work his asshole with gobs of the jelly. It wasn't too long before he relaxed his quivering butthole enough for Frankie to thrust one or two of his fingers inside him. He gasped with exhilaration as he felt the football stud work half his hand up his ass, gently at first, then with a firm upthrust that sent shudders of ecstasy through his asshole.

"Here it comes, stud," said Frankie as he poised the rock-hard tip of his penis against Tommy's waiting butthole.

"Give it to me, Frankie. Be my very first fuck."

Frankie didn't need any more coaxing. Tommy felt the slippery head slide into his ass about an inch and tensed up.

"Just relax," said Frankie as he leaned over and planted hot kisses on the back of Tommy's neck. "Just relax and let it inside. I'll start off slow."

Tommy concentrated on relaxing his insides. He eventually felt confident enough to push back on Frankie's cock, signaling him to continue. They communicated that way for a minute or two until Tommy could feel the entire seven inches of the football stud's cock inside him. It felt full and warm and made him shiver with expectation. He felt impaled on the hunky stud's monster cock, his ass thrusting out like a pair of huge melons waiting to be plucked. Frankie began to pull his cock out, slowly, until it was only halfway in. Then he would pulse his muscular pelvis and drive it deep inside Tommy. His rhythm increased and Tommy felt the huge cock stretch his ass. It sent waves of pleasure through him to feel the man-stud's piston-like movements. He enjoyed feeling the raw desire that the football player dude had for his ass. He soon felt himself grasp the muscular fucker's cock with his ass muscles, squeezing it tightly as it pummeled his bowels. He heard Frank moan and start to really pound his dick inside him then. It wasn't too long before the hunk was exploding inside him, sending stream after stream of hot juicy cum that licked the insides of Tommy's ass. The cum made a squelching sound as Frank continued his thrusts. The obscene noise combined with the smells of sweat and hormones sent Tommy over the edge. He splattered the cubicle wall with erupting cum that splattered and ran down the sides like a silent testimony to his lost virginity. Nothing, no, nothing could have made him happier.

Tommy wiped his ass clean with toilet paper while Frank stuffed his spent member back into his briefs with the bravado of a man who had just had a good fuck. He pulled his pants up over his bulging thighs and gave Tommy a smile.

"See you around on the fifth floor some time, baby!"

Tommy felt flushed with excitement. He finished cleaning himself and pulled up his own pants. Exiting the stall, he went over to the mirrors to check himself out. It was in the mirror that he saw one of the other cubicle doors swing open and his roommate Charlie emerge.

"Heard you two going at it, Tommy-boy! You two really put on a show. Had to jack myself off, it was so hot."

"You mean you...you're...into guys?" Tommy mumbled, completely in shock.

"That's right. I was wondering when you were going to catch on, farm boy. Want to head back to the dorm for some serious sex talk?" Charlie said with a grin.

"Charlie, I never would have guessed. Let's go!"

They left the bathroom together, but not before Charlie laid a lingering smack against Tommy's well-fucked ass. It was an ass that was going to be his tonight.

REST AREA

Chuck Willman

By six o'clock the blazing desert sun was finally beginning to sink behind the jagged ridges of the Spring Mountains west of Las Vegas. The end of August was brutal while the sun was up, and there was barely any relief once its fire was extinguished. But I loved driving in the desert at night. Wearing only a pair of baggy nylon shorts, I tossed my backpack into the backseat, dropped the top of my 1972 convertible VW Bug and pulled onto Highway 15.

For days I had been looking forward to this weekend getaway to Los Angeles to see my Italian buddy, Tony, whom I had met while playing tag-team with a few other horny men in a public toilet. We became insatiable fuckbuddies and good friends as a result, and Tony was up for just about anything. Thinking about it made my cock swell, so I blasted the radio to remain focused on the highway. Soon the warm desert wind slapped me in the face and brushed through the hairs of my chest and armpits. The trickle of sweat running down my neck and over my tits turned me on, and my nipples became hard as stones.

I had chugged an entire liter of water in about half an hour and already needed to take a leak. There was a gas station just a few miles ahead off the highway where I could use the john, pick up some more water and something to munch on. A few minutes later I pulled into the parking lot of the Gas 'N' Go, threw my T-shirt on and headed for the restrooms in the back of the store. The john had two urinals and a toilet with no partitions, crammed in a space the size of a large closet. I was alone and stood at one of the urinals. As I was in mid-stream the door opened and another guy walked in and stood next to me. Standing shoulder to shoulder with me, he unfurled his plump, long penis, which I could clearly see peripherally, and exhaled loudly as his heavy stream pounded against the porcelain. I shook and stuffed myself back into my shorts, then turned around to wash and throw some cold water on my face. I tried to study him more closely from behind in the cracked mirror above the sink.

He was a brawny, blond, bronzed, Nordic-looking stud in cutoff 501s that were so shredded they looked as if they'd unravel if he moved and a stretched-out tank top. When he finished peeing he turned around to rewrap the large package between his legs, and he watched me as I scanned his entire body via the scratched mirror. He had round, firm pecs, broad shoulders, and thick, solid arms with grapefruit-sized biceps, all coated with a luxurious carpet of fine, flaxen hair. My eyes roamed up his muscular, furry legs, arriving at the worn-out threads of his button fly. Half the buttons were either missing or left undone, and hairs that looked like soft corn silk spilled out. A smile leaked through his scruffy golden beard, and his soft green eyes held me in a trance. "Where ya headed?" he asked.

"L.A." I answered.

"Same here!" he replied with a grin.

"I'm Jake," he said, extending his gigantic hand and shaking mine with a powerful grip.

"Chris," I replied. "Good to meet you."

We stood silently for a few seconds, blatantly looking each other over before he reached for the door to leave. "Catch ya later man," he said.

I grabbed a large bottle of water and watched his hard bubble-butt practically split the seams of his worn-out shorts as he walked out of the store. I drooled imagining what his naked ass looked like! I hadn't expected to see anything like that in the Gas 'N' Go! But I had to gear up for the rest of my drive. I peeled my T-shirt off again, hopped into my Bug and raced back onto the highway thinking of Jake's hot body.

About a half hour passed and I was horny again as the thick, long hairs in my armpits and around my nipples blew in the warm breeze. My thoughts locked on the vision of hot, hairy Jake, and my cock started to rise, making my khaki nylon shorts look like a pup tent. Not more than two minutes later a pickup truck raced by me. I looked over quickly to see Jake smiling broadly. He wasn't wearing his tank top, and his massive, glistening chest was accentuated by the bronze light of the sunset pouring in through his windshield. I had to force myself to shift my eyes back to the highway in front of me. He remained locked at my side, driving down the desolate highway for a couple of minutes. And he didn't seem to mind at all that I was ogling him.

Cruising along right next to me, he shouted, "Hey!" through his open window, shifting his eyes between me and the road. "I told you I'd run into you!" He flashed his sexy grin again.

I smiled back and nodded. Then he suddenly accelerated and turned into my lane, right in front of me. This short game of tease brought my cock to full attention. I reached into my shorts to scoop up the pool of precome, rubbing my sticky fingers over my stiff nipples, which made them tingle as my syrup cooled in the rushing air. We continued for several miles. The highway was virtually abandoned with only a few cars passing us from the opposite direction. The sun was almost entirely hidden behind the mountains, so every vehicle had its headlights on, and mine were shining almost right into the cab of Jake's little Toyota truck about thirty yards ahead of me. At one point I realized he was holding up the pair of denim shorts he had been wearing, tossing them on the seat next to him. He was driving naked and the thought made my mouth water!

Jake flashed his right turn signal as we passed a sign that read: REST AREA- 2 MILES. I flashed my headlights back at him, like an automatic reflex. I had no idea where these coded messages would take me, but I was more than eager to find out. Jake turned off the highway and into the rest area, parking his truck near the stucco building that housed the toilets. I followed his lead and pulled into a spot next to him, and took a deep breath. We were the only people there. I got out of my car trying to wrestle my swollen cock down, and slowly walked over to Jake's truck.

Jake opened his door and stood up, completely naked, rubbing his chiseled, hairy body. "How's it goin'?" he purred, grinning from ear to ear.

"Not bad," I answered, swallowing hard. "And you?"

"Ah, man! Much better now!"

"Do you drive like this all the time?" I asked, clasping my hands in front of me to shield my cock that was trying to break through my nylon shorts.

He looked down at himself, scratched his belly and raked his thick patch of pubic hair through his fingers. "Like what?"

"Naked!" I laughed. We were at least seventy or eighty yards from the highway, and there were only small lights over the parking lot and sidewalks. Joshua trees and cactus scraped the sky, and a few bushes were scattered around. It was barren enough to see anything or anyone approaching, and the deep blue haze of dusk made his naked, muscular body glow.

"It feels great!" he answered. "Does it bother you?"

"Hell, no!" I snapped defensively. "I've just never driven naked."

"You know what they say," he said as he began fondling his balls. "Don't knock it 'til you've tried it!" Then he stood defiantly, crossing his arms.

I accepted the dare and yanked my shorts and sandals off, tossing them into my car. The warm air felt great as it blew over my balls and the crack of my ass, and my engorged cock surged freely. Jake was a bold, appealingly smug motherfucker who obviously knew how to have a good time. I knew Tony would understand if I showed up in L.A. a little late. In fact he'd expect a full, detailed report of the encounter. Besides, I assumed this wasn't going to be a quick blow job in a toilet stall.

Jake began stroking his thick shaft with one hand while tugging on his nuts with the other. Then he gathered both of his balls and stretched them farther down his leg, banging them against his thighs like the clapper of a giant bell, making his cock smack against his ripped belly. My mouth watered as he slammed his enormous balls against his legs, and I knew I wanted to get them in my mouth. With his prick and heavy nuts bobbing between his legs, Jake quietly walked backward, stopping once he reached a cement picnic table. I followed him as if he were some kind of magnet. He hopped up on the smooth top of the concrete slab and spread his legs wide open. I honed in on his dark patch of pubic hair and snorted my way to the balls he held tightly in his fist.

"You wanna suck on my nuts, don't you?" he purred, as he played with them.

"Oh, yeah," I stuttered as I moved in closer.

"You sure?" he teased.

"Anything you want!" I begged, wagging my tongue like a ravenous dog.

He grinned and leaned back on the table, bending his knees and propping his muscular torso up on one elbow. "Suck 'em!" he barked, strangling his nuts tightly in place for me. I dropped to my knees and rolled my tongue over his balls. Then I stuffed them completely into my mouth. My eyes watered as I gagged, and saliva ran down my chin. He pulled them from my mouth and let them hang freely between his legs. His wet, hairy, heavy sac reached all the way down to the dark cleft of his ass. "Eat my ass!" he ordered, spreading his legs and hoisting his balls up to expose his succulent asshole. I flicked my tongue over the satiny skin of his chute surrounded by locks of golden hair. His musty scent and taste drove me wild, and I licked along the crack of his ass until every hair was soaked with my spit. He groaned in ecstasy as my tongue burrowed its way into his hole. "Fuck, yeah! Eat my pig hole!"

I pushed his legs back and buried my face in his crack, suckling and chewing on his big, pink pucker. I felt like an animal feeding, and I savored every minute of it. I rubbed my lips all around his sweet asshole, my goatee mopping up his taste and scent, and watched his slimy asshole blink at me when I came up for air.

The sudden bright flash of headlights startled me, and I stopped for a moment. A semi-truck roared off the highway, finally parking in the large gravel big-rig area behind us. The lights hadn't hit us directly, but I was pretty sure our pale bodies were visible against the darkness. Jake was still sliding up and down the cement table begging me to tongue-fuck him harder, oblivious to anything else, so I resumed my feeding position between the cheeks of his fuzzy ass.

A few minutes later, between Jake's squeals and moans, I heard footsteps on the hard ground near us. I didn't pay any attention to them at first, until I noticed the eighteen-wheeler was dark and silent. I scanned the area around us, but didn't see anyone. So I went back to French-kissing Jake's asshole, reaching up to pinch his big, erect nipples until he squirmed and grunted even more. From the corner of my eye, I saw something move about ten yards from us behind a cluster of bushes. Reluctantly, I pulled away from Jake's ass. When the figure finally moved closer I could see a bald, stocky man wearing only black motorcycle boots. It had to be the truck driver since there were no other vehicles around, and he must have been standing there for a while watching us. I liked an audience, and I hoped he wasn't going to just stand off in the distance and watch. Jake continued to grind his beefy, velvety butt into my face. So I drilled my tongue back into his hot ass, ignoring our spectator.

The trucker moved in closer. He was a burly, middle-aged guy completely blanketed with hair. He rubbed the big knob of his hefty prick and pinched his tits as he slowly stepped forward. Jake finally turned his head when he heard the footsteps creeping closer in the rocky sand. He studied the man carefully, and then positioned himself across the width of the table to hang his head off the end. Then Jake opened his mouth.

The trucker stepped up to Jake's inverted face and stuffed his fat meat down Jake's throat, growling as Jake gagged on its girth. But Jake managed to swallow the cock whole, right down to the hairy nuts that smashed his nose. The trucker fucked Jake's mouth deep and hard with his thick, veined cock while I worked Jake's asshole open with my fingers, making way for my tongue to burrow even farther into his delicious cave. "Man! You've got a hot mouth!" the trucker said, beaming, watching Jake suck down the entire length of his tool hungrily. The trucker grabbed Jake's ankles, pulling them toward him, which made Jake's ass spread completely, allowing me to drag my long tongue slowly up and down the length of his crack and feast on his hole. "I got 'em for ya," he said. "I think I'd like a taste of that hole myself!" He pulled his spit-soaked cock from Jake's mouth.

We traded places. The trucker began mopping up Jake's gooey crack with his thick mustache, and I shoved my boner into his mouth. While Jake sucked my cock deep into his throat, I leaned down and took his between my lips, gnawing on the head before sliding the pecker completely into my throat. My face met with the trucker's as he lapped at the soft, pink flesh of Jake's hole. The trucker offered his mouth for me to taste, and our tongues wrapped themselves into a deep kiss. His lips were soft and full, and he kissed me roughly, licking my mouth and chin until he had slurped up the remains of Jake's sweet ass-honey.

"I think he needs a good fuckin'!" the trucker announced, thumping his cock against the crack of Jake's ass. "I wanna plug this big fucker into your hole!"

Jake enthusiastically rocked back and forth while the back of his throat continued to clamp down on my prick.

The trucker opened Jake's hole with two of his pudgy fingers. "Nice! We got you good and wet!" he growled.

I pulled Jake's balls aside to see the trucker line up the head of his stiff, thick meat against Jake's yawning asshole. Without warning he rammed his cock into Jake in one, merciless thrust.

His mouth still full of me, Jake tried to let out a squeal and lay still on the table. After savoring the initial pain of being impaled, Jake went back to sucking my cock even harder as the trucker slammed his hefty prick into Jake's chute. I wrapped a hand around Jake's oozing, twitching cock. He groaned and looked like he was sinking into the concrete table and I knew he could explode at any moment.

I knew it wouldn't take much more for me to blow my nuts either. "Fuck! I'm gonna come!" I screamed.

The trucker looked up to me, sweat pouring from his face. "Me too!"

Jake seized his dick from my hand and pumped it hard in his own fist. I pulled my cock out of his mouth and cradled my balls. The trucker pulled his slimy meat from Jake's ass and stroked it with his large hand. "I want both of you to blow your load on me!" Jake screamed, beating his cock harder. His legs were still spread wide with his knees drawn up.

"Let's give him what he wants!" the trucker said.

Jake pumped his cock as we stood over him. My entire body shook as I felt my come churn. "I'm gonna come!" I yelled.

"Let it go, buddy!" the trucker bellowed in a guttural roar.

Jake begged, "Spray it!"

I threw my head back and my dick erupted, blasting thick ropes of semen all over Jake and hitting the trucker's hairy barrel chest. It kept shooting out in powerful spurts, almost knocking me back. As I was coming, the trucker shot his wad, spreading his white cream all over Jake's stomach and chest. Then Jake heaved as he blew his nuts all over himself, the warm globs of his sperm blending with ours into huge glistening puddles from his neck down to his bush. Each strand of hair on the thick forest covering Jake's torso sparkled with the mix of sweat and come. He finally let his legs drop over the edge of the table, trying to catch his breath.

"Fuck me!" Jake exclaimed, gasping and obviously satisfied.

"Give me a few minutes and I'll pound you again!" laughed the trucker. "You got a hot ass, and your mouth ain't bad either!"

I caught my balance and breath. "Damn! I sure as hell didn't expect this kind of action out here!"

Jake winked. "I'm glad I could show you one of my favorite spots."

The trucker grinned at both of us. "I don't mean to come and go," he snickered, "but I really need to get back on the road."

"Thanks for pulling in...literally!" Jake laughed.

"Anytime, man!" the trucker replied, staggering toward his truck. He faded back into the darkness and was soon out of sight.

I looked at my watch and realized how late I was going to be getting into L.A. "I gotta take off, too."

Jake stood up slowly, letting the thick rivers of our sperm drip from his body onto the ground. "I'm glad I ran into you. Maybe I'll see you around?"

"I sure as hell hope so!" I answered.

We walked back to the parking lot, our bodies illuminated by the bright moon. I didn't even throw my shorts or T-shirt on when I reached my car. It felt good being naked outdoors. I watched as the trucker climbed back into the cab of his rig still naked, despite being parked under a light, and Jake got back into his pickup truck, also naked. We all smiled and nodded to each other. Then they both zoomed back onto the highway, a trail of dust following them.

I decided to enjoy the solitude for a while longer. Naked and alone, I sprawled myself out on the hood of my car. I thought about the two hairy studs that just left, all of us yelping and grunting as we ravaged each other and shot our loads. I could still smell Jake on my goatee, tasting him as I licked my whiskers. My cock sprang straight up again as I envisioned his butthole. I started jerking off, cupping my balls in my other hand. And even though I had just emptied them minutes earlier, warm gobs of jizz spilled out of my prick and onto my belly. I could have slept right there under the stars, but I knew Tony was waiting for me. At least I'd have a couple more hours on the highway to rest up for the next round with him!

I got back into my Bug and continued heading west with the soothing desert air washing over me as I drove—naked for a change. It was as close to Heaven as I could imagine. I couldn't wait to tell Tony all about it and make another stop at this rest area on my way home.

ONE HOT BABY

Daniel Curzon

This is a true story. That doesn't make it true, of course. It was something that happened just one time, never before and never since, and never again. I don't mean to make it sound like a riddle. Yet it was a riddle, sort of. I don't think it changed my life. Well, maybe a little.

I was on my way home from work. I'm a claims adjuster. I should have retired a long time ago, I suppose, but I didn't and haven't, mainly because I like my job. Oh, it's boring at times and people lie like mad trying to fool my insurance company. I suppose I enjoy catching them. I was going to be a lawyer, or so I thought, and yet somehow that never worked out. I would have been a prosecutor. You know why? Because the real problem today is not that innocent people are convicted for crimes they didn't commit. It's the crimes committed that never get punished! Where's the outcry over that? Just last week there was this fellow—I won't say where he was from. Let's just say it wasn't from America!—who was trying to screw the hell out of my company, claiming his grandmother was entitled to money from the accident he was in because—get this!—she wasn't able to move here to the States the way he'd been planning because now she said Americans were dangerous drivers and she was afraid to come after his accident, an accident that he caused!

But don't get me started.

I was on my way home and needed to take a leak so bad I could taste it. It had been a very bad day. My boss, who is forty (I'm seventy-two) chewed me out for not filling out some form properly, something I've done for fifty-one years. The worst part is that he was right. I think my memory is going a little bit. I really should retire, but what am I going to do, sit around and twiddle my fingers? My friend Frank complains all the time that he is bored out of his mind. He has taken up babysitting some feral cats behind his house and going to a shabby mall twice a day just to have something to do.

Anyway, it was not a good day—it was yesterday I'm talking about. I got a haircut at the barbershop next door to my office during my lunch break, and as I sat in the barber chair with all this awful hair from other customers littering the floor—Gus won't sweep it up except once a day; claims he's too busy; I tell him it looks awful—I looked, really looked, at my reflection in the mirrors. Gus has several of them on both sides of his shop, so there's no escaping what you look like. And I noticed that I'm really starting to age. I've always looked younger than I am, by a good ten years. Only yesterday I could see the bald spot in the back that I usually can't see in the mirror in my bathroom. If you don't have to see, why look for it, right? Well, here it was, with all this gray hair around it, some of it sticking up on the left side even though I had wetted it down that morning. It made me look like a jerk. Next to my right eye I could see an age spot coming through, and they're coming through on the backs of my hands too. Yeah, yeah, the Golden Years, my ass! It's Death rotting you from the inside out. There were also pouches under my eyes too, not huge ones, but I never used to have pouches! The skin on my face looked loose. This is what I get for losing thirty pounds by eating goddamn low-calorie breadsticks and steamed cauliflower for the last six months? Now I've got loose skin that puts on at least ten years! The hair grows in my ears too, and now it's not only too long, it's gray.

So I'm sitting there looking at myself, and Gus, who's bony and Greek and ninety if he's a day, says to me, "You been sick, Artie?"

I didn't answer him. And I didn't give him a tip either. He gives lousy haircuts, always has. I don't know why I keep going there.

"You look hunched over," Gus goes on, as if I'm there for a beauty consultation. This from a guy who practically invented osteoporosis himself! "You need some calcium, Artie," he tells me.

"Yeah, yeah," I says. "Why don't you clean up the fucking hair off the floor!"

He didn't talk to me after that. Which left no small talk, the way we usually talk, and I just had to sit there and stare at my seventy-two-year-old face, trying not to think of the less-than-stellar man-boobs that have come in during the past few years. Or the gorilla nipples. Or the softening and drooping of that area above the cock, below the belly button. But you get the picture. I don't have to draw you one.

Sure, it's natural. Nature sucks.

Anyhoo, I'm driving home having to take a leak like there's no tomorrow, and I drive by this park. I've driven by it a million times before. I don't bother going there. Let's face it, I'm not a great hiker, barely a walker. It's getting dark because it's close to winter, and there's no restroom in the park, I'm pretty sure, because they closed it, I read.

So I parked my car to relieve myself of the two diet Pepsis I'd had to keep on my diet, and I went up this little path with all these cypress trees alongside it, some vegetation—don't ask me to name it. I'm terrible at flowers and stuff like that. It was pretty dense because we've had a lot of rain this year.

I thought I wasn't going to make it and might actually pee in my pants.

You probably don't want to hear about it, but that's happened to me a few times recently. Just couldn't hold it. The old prostate is kicking the bucket, my doctor says. Not cancer, thank god, just ENLARGED. (Get it? Enlarged?)

Somehow I managed to whip the old wiener out despite the goddamn pinching zipper and the fucking underwear. There I am standing spewing like the god of urine, whoever that is, and feeling so lucky to be a guy and not having to squat to piss. I must have uncorked a quart, if it was an ounce. "Thank you, God!" I said under my breath. I say that every time I have a good pee these days. The stupid Flomax isn't all it's cracked up to be. And I forget to take it sometimes, I have to admit.

So I'm putting away the old equipment and I notice this young guy standing there halfway behind a tree. He's about thirty, slender, with a little mustache. I think his hair was dark brown. I know it was short. He was wearing just regular clothes—pants, jacket, I couldn't even say what color they were. Gray, the jacket was gray. Oh, and he was wearing a black and orange baseball cap. Whatever.

I notice that he's half looking at my dick, or at least the crotch. Well, guys just don't do that, I'm here to tell you! I started to say something to him, but he turned away. So I turned away too, having some more trouble with that zipper, while heading back to my car.

And then for some reason I stopped. I could lie and say it was to enjoy the night air, but actually it was getting more than a little cold. I could say I stopped to smell the roses, but those flowers around me out there weren't roses. I know that much.

Then suddenly this guy was back in sight. He looked right into my eyes.

I didn't look away. We both waited to see what was what. I thought I knew what he might be there for, but I didn't know for sure. I mean, he wasn't queeny or anything, and he didn't point to his butt. Isn't that what they do? How would I know?

He was very cautious and took his time. I just sort of stood there with my fingers on my zipper. I felt sort of silly, to be honest, and I almost left.

But I didn't.

After a while, the guy sauntered over and checked me out. It was getting dark and I suppose the bad light did me a good turn. He was most interested in my crotch, but he did look right into my face too. And he didn't turn and run, the way I thought he would. In fact, he got down on his knees, slowly, turned his cap around, and began sucking my wiener like he was no vegetarian, let me tell you! I filled up his mouth, and I didn't even need my Viagra. I watched his head going back and forth. He was really into it. It did not last very long, but it didn't have to at that rate.

"Thank you, God!" I called out as I was coming, not too loud, just a little bit, and he took it all, every drop, every seventy-two-year-old drop in me. And when he got up from his knees and looked me in the face again, he smiled and said the nicest words I probably have ever heard in my whole life: "You're one hot baby." And, no, he wasn't being sarcastic, asshole! He meant it.

Was it the greatest day of my life? No. Was it the greatest day of the past five years and probably the next five years? Probably.

And then he went his way, and I went mine, like ships in the night. The Cocksucker and one hot baby. Thank you, God.

I don't think I'll tell my wife this story.

PHOTO FINISH

Jeremy Andrews Windsor

Dana thought I was nuts. "Azaleas and dogwoods?"

"They're in full bloom. Gorgeous! Come with me."

He shrugged and went back to channel surfing. "No thanks. Tell the birds and bees I said hi, but I'm staying under my warm blankie."

Fine. At least walking through the arboretum alone, I wouldn't hear nagging if I spent too much time lining up the perfect shot. I don't know why I even bothered to ask him along anyway. If it weren't for our mutual interest in saving on rent, and the fact he likes to cook but hates to clean and vice versa, I doubt we'd be living together. After two steamy sessions in the shower after we first moved in together, we barely made eye contact anymore. Friends called us an old married couple. We were more like spinster sisters always getting on each other's nerves.

Thanks to accessing that shower memory file, though, I started to get hard as I waited at the crosswalk for six assholes to speed past the STOP FOR PEDESTRIANS sign. Sex with Dana had been good, I had to admit; he edged me a record six times before I pulled out my cock and shot my load all over his cute face. If I wasn't determined to get some good photos for my portfolio, and if Dana and I were actually still fucking each other, I might have turned around right then, raced back to the apartment and pulled him into the bathroom. But I forced myself to be a good boy, and I crossed Lake Washington Boulevard with all artistic seriousness.

As I hurried to escape another speeding moron, I heard a second pair of feet behind me. I laughed at myself thinking Dana had decided to join me after all. I glanced over my shoulder and saw a hunky Asian dude. The sleeves of his plaid shirt were rolled up just so to highlight his biceps. His hands were tucked into the pockets of his tight jeans. He nodded and gave me a sly smirk, then cut right and started for the path under the bridge.

Yeah, okay, I knew this part of the arboretum was cruisy, but I wasn't in a cruising mood. I had to focus on my art. Besides, I doubted this guy had any interest in me. I felt sure he'd prefer hooking up with one of the buff sunbathers to seducing a geek carrying a digital camera.

Guess I was wrong. As soon as I passed the bridge columns and walked up the pathway, I saw him leaning against a tree about twenty feet ahead of me. His shirt was open. He was massaging his nipple with one hand and fingering his crotch with the other. He smiled. I smiled. He motioned me over with a sexy tilt of the head.

I usually don't go hurrying over to half-naked strangers no matter how tempting, but three things were going on: first, I was horny as hell from shower-scene flashbacks; second, this guy was smoking hot; and third, going down on each other's cocks in a natural setting seemed like the perfect fusion of beauty and lust. As an *artiste*, I had to appreciate that, right?

His smile grew even sexier the closer I moved toward him. He didn't wait for me to walk up; he met me halfway, and I could feel his breath on my face as he took hold of my wrist and placed my hand on his pecs. Guess he had his own shower-scene flashbacks making him just as horny.

I figured I'd get one of the standard questions in this case:

What are you into?

You a cop?

You got someplace we can go?

Instead, he led me behind a clump of trees where hundreds of knees had cleared away the grass and packed down the soil so it was as hard as cement.

"You're cute, man," he said. "What's your name?"

"Mike."

"I'm Corey."

Corey. It sounded so...cliché. "Are you *really* Corey?"

"If I was lying I'd come up with a better name than that."

I smiled. Before I could comment, he squeezed my hard-on.

"You like getting sucked?" he asked.

"Yeah," I whispered back as he started to undo my belt. I leaned over and set my camera at the base of a tree. He pulled down my zipper and tugged open my jeans as I ran my hands up and down his smooth chest.

He nuzzled my neck. I shoved my hands inside his back pockets. His ass was beautifully formed. The scent of his shampoo wafted up as he bent down and peeled back my boxers to reveal the tip of my cock. As he took it into his mouth, I saw some branches move. I tensed.

A young red-haired guy took a couple of steps toward us. He was dressed in black pants, a black vest and white shirt. I guessed he might be a waiter either going to or coming from work. His was stroking one of the biggest cocks I'd ever seen.

This was threesome material. Confession: I'd never experienced a threesome. What to do? Invite him over? Just let him watch? Tell him to scram?

Corey tugged my jeans down to my knees. He kissed the tip of my cock, then slowly moved his plump lips down my shaft. I moaned and took hold of his muscular arms. The redhead got brave and moved closer to us. He undid a couple of buttons of his shirt. He took a couple more steps. Before I knew it, he was standing next to me. He leaned over and planted his lips on mine. Our tongues touched.

Corey grabbed both our cocks. He gently squeezed them together and wrapped his lips around both. Red and I moaned at the same time. I pushed my tongue farther into Red's mouth. He lifted up my shirt and ran his finger over my left nipple with a featherlight touch. It was sweet torture.

Red slid my shirt off. He kissed me again as he massaged my chest. Corey stood up and took his shirt off. His muscles rippled. I glided the tip of my tongue over his tit then sucked on it. He undid his jeans and pulled out his hard-on. He pressed my head closer to his chest. It was warm and smooth and smelled like soap and cologne and sweat. He nudged Red's head down toward his shaft. Red swallowed his cock.

"Fuck," he whispered. "Fuck, yeah."

"Cum in my mouth," Red said. "I wanna swallow your load."

"No, man, not yet." He pulled his cock out of Red's mouth. "I want both you guys to shoot on my face."

More flashbacks to the Dana shower scene! I wouldn't have imagined I could get even more turned on than I already was. It was like Corey had just read my mind. There's nothing that drives me wilder than giving a cute guy a facial. And now I was about to shoot my load all over a hot Asian, my warm cum mixing with a red-hot redhead's.

"Get on either side of me," Corey said. Red walked over to the right, and I moved closer to Corey as he lay down on the ground. Red and I both knelt down next to him. Corey stroked his cock while Red and I leaned in and let him swallow us again.

Red reached down and started fingering Corey's balls. I, in turn, couldn't keep my hands off his chest.

"Cum at the same time, all over my face."

I was getting close. Red looked at me for a signal. I nodded a couple of times.

"Yeah, man, I wanna feel it on me."

I couldn't hold back anymore. The cum was at the tip of my cock, waiting for escape. I put my right hand on Red's chest while Corey gently licked my balls. "I'm gonna cum."

"Yeah, man, all over me."

I glanced at Red to check his status. His face muscles tightened. He stroked faster and faster. Just as a few drops of my precum landed on Corey's chin, Red moaned and titled his head back. It was a direct hit: his jizz landed squarely on those plump Asian lips. I was trying to hold back just a little longer, but seeing those beautiful white drops on Corey's hot lips, I let loose. I shot all over his neck and chin. His nose. His hair.

"Yeah, shit, yeah! Look at all that cum!"

Corey lifted his back off the ground. He gripped his cock, tugged on it harder and harder, exhaling and moaning, his fist slapping against his skin. He writhed as he licked his lips. "Fuck!"

His warm cum flew straight up to his forehead. Several drops landed on his chest. Red leaned down and licked them up.

"Oh, my god," Corey whispered, his eyes still closed.

After taking a few seconds to catch his breath, Red gave us

both a quick peck good-bye, then stood, zipped up and hurried away.

"Sometimes they don't linger," Corey said, running his fingertips along my thigh.

I stroked his arm. "I'm glad *you* did."

"Yeah?"

"You're amazingly hot."

"You wanna hook up again sometime?"

"Ah, you'll forget all about me."

He took his cell phone out of his pocket. He opened it up, pointed it at me and snapped a picture.

"Hey," I said, "no posting that on the web."

He smiled. "Nah, it's to prove that I'm not gonna forget about you." He closed the phone and stashed it back in his jeans. "And to use when I get horny and need something hot to jerk off to."

I glanced at my camera. "I get one too, then."

"Nope."

"Hey, no fair."

He leaned over, picked up my camera and handed it to me. "You have to take a pic of the two of us together."

I smirked as I turned on the camera. I lay down next to him, our arms touching, his olive skin a nice complement to my milky complexion. Our heads touched, and I took two shots of us. "Cute."

"I want a copy."

"Deal."

He kissed me. "Guess what?"

"Huh?"

"I'm getting hard again."

I was too.

As Corey rolled on top of me, my camera switched to video mode. It wasn't intentional. I swear! But, heck, when the two of us came in each other's mouths, you couldn't ask for a more magical moment to be captured on film.

After I showed the footage to Dana later that night, he asked to see it a second time. Then, he suggested we take a shower.

"With or without the camera?" I asked.

Dana took my hand. He led me down the hallway. "Hey," he whispered, "*you're* the director."

ON THE BATHROOM FLOOR

Ryan Field

When the weather is warm I like to jog at a small state park on the outskirts of town, where it's thick with tall, green cedar trees; where the wildflowers dot the hills with colors of the rainbow in spring and where extremely horny straight guys stop to use the restrooms on their way to work. It doesn't happen every morning; about two or three times a month is enough to create a certain anticipation of great pleasure so that the jogging itself never becomes repetitive. I go there to work out and sucking cock is simply the occasional fringe benefit. It's a beautiful park, with paved walking trails and open pavilions and a Pennsylvania stone restroom haphazardly glazed in lime-green moss.

This place is frequented often by guys wearing jeans and work boots, driving huge, extended-cab pickup trucks on their way to construction jobs. Married men in dark suits that smell like aftershave, driving four-door Japanese sedans on their way to office jobs in the city come, too. Men of all ages and from all walks of life who stop to use the restrooms and see what's happening on the down low. Some are only interested in whipping their dicks out for a quick piss, and others are furtively looking for a little fast morning action on their way to work. It's not that this is a known cruise spot by any means. Admittedly, half the fun is in distinguishing who is looking for action and who just wants to release a load of piss.

One morning last May, an unusually warm, humid day for late spring, I was just finishing a four-mile run when I noticed a cable van pull up to the restroom. A typical white van, with ladders and equipment fastened to the roof and the cable-TV logo painted on the sides. It had been about three weeks since I'd seen any men pull up to the restroom at the same time when I jog so I decided to watch very closely. Through foggy side windows I could see there was only one cable guy in the van that morning (sometimes they travel in pairs, which can be awkward). I knew he'd seen me jogging the path when he pulled into the park, but it was too soon to know if he was cruising or simply stopping to pee.

The driver's side door opened and a stocky guy in his early twenties stepped down from the van and walked toward the heavy restroom door. He was medium height, had a large frame and his hair was cut very short. Black work boots, white painter's pants and a plain white T-shirt; all very clean and ready to begin a new day. Without turning he walked into the restroom, unaware that I was watching every move, and let the door slam.

I waited a few minutes, walking back and forth in front of my own car, cooling down from the run and counting the minutes since he'd entered the restroom. If he were only there to piss I knew he'd be out in less than three minutes, and going into the restroom for me would just be a waste of time.

Four minutes later, though I still wasn't certain he was there to cruise, I suspected it might be worth my while to go inside and see what was happening. I opened the metal door and entered the dark, musty building I knew so well. There was a short hall, and then a quick turn to the left that led to the main men's room where there were three gray graffiti-covered stalls, two rust-streaked, piss-stained, urinals and one small sink with only cold running water. A narrow row of dirty windows allowed some natural light, but all you could see were branches and leaves when you looked up. With a quick glance, I saw that the cable guy was sitting on a toilet in one of the stalls, his pants around his ankles and his right hand holding his big cock. The door to the stall was slightly ajar, a signal that he was in no rush. But I still couldn't be certain that he was cruising or that the situation was totally safe. I knew that some guys just like to get off alone, and if they are disturbed it could get violent. Had he opened the door, spread his hairy legs and pointed toward his cock I would have been on my knees sucking him off right at the toilet. But he didn't do that, and one of my rules for cruising the restroom was that I'd never make the first obvious move toward the other guy. No matter how horny I was. However, there were certain things I could do to get his attention and to let him know that I was interested.

Though I couldn't see him completely, I knew full well that he could see every move I made. So I decided to put on a small show. At thirty-two years old, after working out and running most of my life, my body is in good shape. My legs are long and lean, my waist only thirty inches and my chest is pumped up to a full forty-three inches. My ass is round and firm and smooth due to the fact that I shave everything, except for a small, dark-blond patch in the shape of an upside-down triangle above my dick, every three days. When I jog in the summer months I only wear running shoes, a tight pair of Lycra shorts and a loose-fitting tank top. Though I know I'll never have bulging muscles, I am lean and firm and have an eight-inch dick that flops around nicely when it is soft and stands firmly with a slight upward curve when hard.

Without hesitation, I slowly began to remove my running shoes, and then my socks, in total silence. From the corner of my eye I saw the door of the stall where he was sitting. I then pulled off my tank top and yanked off my running shorts, placing them neatly in a pile on top of the paper towel dispenser to my right. I then ran the palms of my hands through my damp blond hair and stretched, sucking in my waist and arching my back. Now totally nude, standing in the middle of a public men's room, I walked toward the sink and splashed some cold water on my face. Though bold, this wasn't out of the ordinary, and by no means illegal...yet. I was in a men's room, where only men were supposed to be, a sacred place for men to change clothes or wash up or use the toilets. I wasn't crossing any lines or doing anything I shouldn't have been doing.

Though the cable guy didn't know this, I could see from the foggy mirror over the old sink that he was watching every move I made, with bulging eyes, while my back was turned to him.

But by that time he should have opened the door and exposed his dick, or stood and made a gesture for me to go down on my knees. I'd learned that all I had to do was take off my pants, show a little ass, and I could get almost any guy to follow me into the woods, so to speak. Clearly, though it was not fully erect, he could see my cock. That, I guess, is when the line is crossed and everyone knows where they stand. You can walk around naked in a men's room and it's perfectly normal if your cock is soft. Maybe I was giving him mixed signals, acting so cool and carefree, not showing signs of a hard dick. So I decided to cross that line and take my chances.

Still standing in front of the sink, I splashed cold water all over my chest and slowly began to rub it into my hot skin, knowing that my cock would reach a full erection. A minute later, with almost nine inches of hard dick, I turned so that he could see everything and walked toward the paper towel dispenser. My cock was so fucking hard by that time I could have pitched a tent. I pulled a rough, brown towel from the metal box and slowly wiped my torso dry. But I didn't touch my dick. I just kept turning in his direction so he wouldn't miss an inch of it.

Yet he still didn't make a move. But as I glanced toward the stall, though not making eye contact, I could see that he was now stroking his dick and watching me at the same time. I figured it might just be a jerk-off show for him, and that he probably wouldn't make a move. I considered going down on the tiled floor, spreading my legs and arching my back, but then thought it might be too obvious. You have to let them know that you like dick, but you can't beg...unless of course they ask for begging.

So I decided to push things and go into the stall next to his, sitting down on the cold, white toilet, stark naked, with all my clothes out in the main area on top of the metal dispenser. However, I decided to leave my door open, a clear invitation. Maybe he'd slide a foot over and give some sort of signal, rub his dirty work boot against my smooth ankle. Some guys are only comfortable behind the safety of a stall. And then I heard the rustle of his pants being pulled up, the toilet being flushed and the cable guy opening the door of the stall. With my door wide open I watched him go to the sink and wash his hands very thoroughly. He then walked toward the paper towel dispenser, as though he were all alone and I wasn't sitting there naked and my clothes weren't on top of the dispenser and my legs weren't spread and my cock wasn't standing in a full erection, to dry his hands. He was rugged and stocky and rather hairy, traits I adore. With large hands, strong arms and a solid body that was all man. I was certain that up close he had one of those thick, beer-can cocks.

By that time I figured he'd jerked off while watching my little strip show and was ready to head back to his van. But after he dried his hands he hesitated for a long moment, turned and walked back toward the urinals. He stood before the left urinal, yanked down his zipper and proceeded to pull out his dick. I didn't hear any piss flowing; he simply stood there holding his dick. This, I knew, was a clear signal for me to make the next move.

So I stood up from the toilet, my cock still fully erect, and slowly walked toward the urinal on the right. We stood there in silence for a while, side by side, never making eye contact but knowing something was about to happen. When I looked down and saw that his cock was large and thick and, indeed, like a beer can, I slowly ran my hands up my torso and began to gently squeeze and pinch my hard, brown nipples. I wanted that big cock and all its juice inside my hole. As I did this he reached out with his right hand and softly ran it down my back, resting it at the top of my ass as I gasped with pleasure. He slowly began to squeeze and fondle my asscheeks; my back arched and my eyes began to roll toward the ceiling. It was a rough hand with many calluses.

I gasped again. "Do whatever you want," I whispered, almost begging.

He did not utter a word. Instead, he stood behind me, wrapped his strong hairy left arm around my thin waist and pulled me toward his warm, fully clothed body. With his right hand he began to rub his thick cock up and down the crack of my ass. I wasn't sure if he was ready to fuck right then and there or not. But he then rested both large hands on my ass and began to run them up my smooth body, squeezing and cupping my chest for a moment, stopping at the top of my shoulders. I felt slight pressure and knew he wanted me to go down on the floor.

Submitting completely, I slowly turned, arched my back, spread my legs wide and went down on my knees.

With both my hands placed on his strong thighs, tugging the fabric of his painter's pants, I opened my mouth and took his cock whole. I went right down to the shaft, tasting his pubic hairs. His balls smelled like salt and vinegar, another trait I adore. The head of his thick cock hit the back of my throat, but I'd learned not to gag—-just swallow and suck—-jerking him off with my lips and my tongue, keeping it wet and slippery like a tight, warm pussy. He cupped my head with both hands and began to face-fuck me hard and fast, pushing me back toward the urinal so that my legs were spread wide and my ass was hitting the white porcelain with each thrust. There was a thick, stainless steel knob about three inches long toward the drain (some type of plumbing bolt that held the piss urinal to the tiled wall) and as he fucked my face my asshole kept hitting it as though it were a hard, stainless steel cock.

His dick pulsed and grew with each thrust and I worked him into a rhythm, knowing he was ready to shoot a full load down my throat. The harder I sucked the more I wanted to eat him. And as he grew closer and the sucking grew more intense he gave one hard shove and the stainless steel bolt went right up my ass. I arched my back and took it as though it were a cock and reached around to grab my dick. As I sucked him off I began to bang my ass hard against the porcelain. As hard as I could ram it, with the thick steel bolt filling my hole.

He began to breath heavy as I held his strong thighs for support. I felt his cock swell, ready to blow a full load down my throat, and I continued to suck with an unwavering rhythm. I knew a good cocksucker never changes the beat when a guy is close to shooting a load for fear of ruining the moment. So many poor guys are forced to jerk themselves off because of bad cocksuckers that can't seem to maintain a constant sucking rhythm.

"Yeah, suck that big dirty dick, bitch," he said in a stage whisper. "You're the best little dick-sucker I've ever seen. Suck it, bitch. Go whore. Ah, fuck. Ah, fuck."

His legs began to quiver and he squeezed my head hard as he began to shoot. I barely had to touch my own cock as the steel bolt plunged deep into my ass and his thick, sweet juice went down my throat: three large loads of wonderful sweet cum. I closed my eyes and shot my own load, slowly swallowing every last drop of his delicious nectar.

He didn't pull his thick cock out right away. He allowed me to gently milk it dry as it began to go flaccid against my tongue. As I softly moaned with pleasure, slowly riding the steel bolt that was still deep in my ass, he began to gently rub the back of my head. His entire body went limp as I continued to carefully milk him clean. And, with absolute certainty, I knew I'd done a very excellent job sucking him off.

When his cock was soft and I'd sucked him dry I released it from my mouth. I then reached for it and put it safely back into his painter's pants and pulled up the zipper for him, knowing I'd probably never see that magnificent cock again. But I took satisfaction in knowing I'd had it once, which is more than a lot of cocksuckers can say. Before he turned to leave I was taken aback when he reached down with his right hand and helped me stand again. He then reached behind and gave me a playful slap on the ass in a show of thanks. And I knew that though I'd probably never see him again, he'd never forget the best blow job of his life.

LITTLE SHOP
OF HUMMERS

Gregory L. Norris

The alley behind the flower shop, Mister Voshnik warned him, was a den of sin and sweat.

"Flowers here, fresh as springtime," Len Voshnik said, narrowing his eyes. "Out there, on the other side of our very own dumpster, *fruit*—though not the kind you'll want to snack on, Seymour."

Seymour Kilkenny shrugged. "Why? Is the fruit rotten?"

"To the core. Now, clean out the back room and be quick about it. You'll be making deliveries of Austin's brilliant creations after you're done dumping all those dead twigs and detritus."

Seymour rolled his eyes toward the crafting table where Austin worked. "*De...?*"

Voshnik clapped his hands together, producing thunder. "I'm not paying you by the word, Seymour. To the mess, meathead!"

Seymour nearly tripped over his own huge feet on his way to the back room. En route, he stole another glance at Austin, the flower shop's lead florist and stylist. *Austin*, with his short blond hair and eyes the color of delphiniums and cornflowers, the richest blue he'd ever seen. At that moment, Austin held gladioli, long pink ones, and handled them with the skill of a surgeon, gently snipping their stems at an angle and arranging them in a tall, clear vase. Seeing the exquisite results drained all the moisture from Seymour's mouth, transferring it into his pants. He felt his cock swell. His balls loosened, itched. Suddenly, it wasn't pink glads in Austin's hands; it was Seymour's dick that felt as big as the flowers.

"Hi there, Seymour," Austin said, flashing a smile that showed a length of perfect white teeth surrounded by moist lips.

That such a magnificent creature could exist in Skid Row didn't seem possible. Austin should be dwelling in marble halls, surrounded by lush gardens of flowers. Right before he walked headlong into the back room's ajar door, banging his nose, Seymour imagined Austin's lips wrapped around his erection. And then the world erupted in a big bang of exploding stars as he and the door collided.

Drooping Easter lilies and desiccated ferns went into the dumpster. Seymour worked up a decent sweat by noon, and had stuffed the dumpster—which also served the club next door, Core Man—full to the top. At that hour, Club Core Man was closed. No rotting grapes or kumquats shared space with the dead flowers in the dumpster. Clearly, Mister Voshnik was hallucinating.

The alley sat empty and still, unlike the front of Seymour's blue jeans. He'd walked around miserable for most of the morning, erect and constricted, his DNA reacting with basic, primitive impulses following Austin's gazes, smiles and maneuvers in and around the refrigerator case full of daffodils and daisies. The tent beneath his zipper was wet at the crown, his dick rubbed almost to the point of busting without so much as a single stroke from his hand. Seymour reached down and adjusted himself. Pins and needles erupted in concentric waves from his junk, rippling down his legs and up his torso. It wouldn't take much to make him nut, and a crotch covered in clots of his seed, he figured, wouldn't play well to the customers of Voshnik's Flower Shop he would soon be delivering arrangements to.

Seymour tipped a look around. Yup, the alley was still empty. Deeming it safe too, he slipped behind the dumpster and unzipped. Freeing his dick from his tight-whites unleashed equal amounts of pain and pleasure. His erection snapped up, looking redder than he'd ever seen it. His balls tumbled out, meaty and loose, dangling, he swore, halfway to his hairy ankles. He drew in a deep breath; the alley's musty odor and the dry, dead smell of former green things recently added to the dumpster filled his lungs. Among the eucalyptus and yucca, he caught a whiff of male sweat, ripe and heady: his own.

"*Austin,*" Seymour moaned.

A dopey smile formed on his face. Spitting on his right palm, he lubed up his shaft and started to jerk it. Seymour's balls bounced. Fresh sweat broke across his forehead, beneath the bill of his backward-turned baseball cap, under his arms, between his toes, which baked in his Keds. Austin, beautiful Austin.

He settled his spine against the dumpster and pumped. The vibrations steadily jostled a cardboard box full of half-dead plants, loose seeds from Japan and Madagascar, and shriveled-up bamboo.

"Austin," he grunted. "Tell me that you love me..."

Only dream-Austin's mouth was too full to speak, and his smile was wrapped around Seymour's cock. The same elegant fingers that normally played around carnations, tulips and lemon leaves yanked on his nuts. Seymour's shoulders tensed.

The box of dead and half-dead flora toppled, bouncing off his head. Seymour jumped. He was close, so fucking close.

"That's right, Austin…yeah, tug on my ball sac. Harder, oh fuck, just like that, babe…"

He fantasized about spinning Austin around, pulling down his pants and plugging him full of dick while bent over the table where he snipped ribbons and designed floral arrangements for weddings, funerals and bar mitzvahs. That did it. Seymour's balls gonged together one last time before pulling up tightly against his root and pumping what felt like a gallon of custard out of his cock. He huffed Austin's name again. Then, Voshnik barked from the other side of the shop's back door.

"Seymour, where are you? I'm paying you to deliver plants, not dither out there among *the fruits!*"

Seymour shook out his cock before tucking everything back into his briefs. "Coming, Mister Voshnik," he answered, wincing at both the statement and the miserable pressure on his dick.

Seymour zipped and hurried away from the dumpster. From the corner of his eye, he caught sight of the massive load he'd sprayed across the spillover. He'd worry about picking up that mess later, after deliveries were made and his pulse stopped racing.

It was well after dark when he made it back to the alley between Voshnik's Flower Shop and Club Core Man. By then, Voshnik's was closed, but the club was filling up with patrons. A band played a cover of "Saturday Night Special," only to Seymour it sounded more like a Sunday morning hangover.

He moseyed up to the dumpster. In the poor light, he made out the cardboard box, which had since been trampled. A musky sweetness infused the air.

"Fruit?" Seymour wondered out loud.

Without warning, two men shuffled out of the shadows.

"I don't much care for that word," one said, wiping his mouth.

The other, a clean-cut dude dressed in a crisp white dress shirt, thin black tie and dark suit got up into Seymour's face. "Yeah, who do you think you are, judging us, you hater."

Seymour held up both hands. "I wasn't hating or judging, man—I'm just here to clean up the mess I left all over the place."

Suit-dude backed off, chuckled and adjusted his package. "Then you came to the right place. Old Gravis here is really good at slurping up the spooge, down to the last drop."

The lip-licker playfully smacked suit-dude's wrist. "Oh, hush, Wilberforce."

The two men continued on, past the dumpster and toward the growing crowd outside the club's back door, arm in arm. Jealousy surged through Seymour's blood. If only he and Austin were that close, that committed. If only—

"*Feed me,*" crooned a weak voice from somewhere close by.

Seymour scanned the shadows.

"*Feed me...*"

He glanced down toward the ground, expecting to see a face, perhaps one of Gravis or Wilberforce's fellow club patrons. Among the desiccated remains of the dead plants he'd pitched into the dumpster, he made out a weak smile, only it wasn't human, and it didn't belong to a face in the traditional sense. Two pale pink lips wreathed in frail vegetation stared up at him. If the thing had had real eyes, Seymour imagined they would have pleaded for his help.

"You poor thing," he said, reaching down, scooping the half-alive flower back into the pot of powdered soil it had spilled out of. He lifted it up until its lips and his eyes were even. In the poor light, he made out dark veins pulsing through its delicate flesh and detected the bitter stink of a man's musk—he'd nailed it with one of his ropes of sperm, judging by the glistening streaks across its mouth.

The lips trembled. Seymour reached toward them, intending to offer comfort. Instead, the plant's mouth gently sucked his pointer finger down to the bottom knuckle.

The inside of those lips was surprisingly wet, warm and wonderful. The plant nursed on his finger. Seymour half closed his eyes and pretended it was Austin, stunning Austin, at work on him and his dick, not his finger, receiving the attention.

"Feed me, *please*," the plant begged around his finger.

In his shock, Seymour almost dropped the plant. "You...you can speak!"

The lips drooped and leaves sagged in response, the plant obviously stressed from its brief though arousing effort. It was beyond thirsty, its roots clutching at desert. Seymour tried the back door to Voshnik's, but it was locked. He needed to water the plant as soon as possible, or it would die.

"*Feed...*"

He shifted in place, shocked to discover that his cock was back up to its earlier stiffness.

"*...me!*"

"Okay, hold on," he said, fumbling his jeans open, one-handed. His cock jutted out. Seymour tucked the elastic waistband of his underwear beneath his balls, smelling more of his funky scent in the updraft. He lowered the lips toward his cock. The plant's mouth latched on, tentatively at first, its movements light as whispers over his dick's straining knob. But then its mouth tightened and engulfed Seymour's cockhead fully, firmly. Something tickled his nuts. Peering down, he saw that it was a vine and several leaves, working in concert like a rudimentary hand.

"Oh, my...*fuck*," Seymour huffed.

The mouth hummed around his cock, its happy vibrations sending electricity down his shaft, along the sensitive patch of skin between his nuts and his asshole. Seymour closed his eyes fully this time and, in his imagination, it was Austin he saw so happily doling out what he agreed was the best head of his life.

"Oh Austin, *Austin*," groaned Seymour.

Austin was sucking him, the florist's mouth wrapped around his straining dick after weeks of driving Seymour mad every time he raised a pink carnation or rosebud to his nostrils for a sniff. Seymour's toes curled in his sneakers. He flexed them, pushed in deeper. The mouth greedily accepted. Every inch of Seymour's flesh ignited.

He unloaded into the plant's mouth, squirting a quantity equal to what he'd dumped earlier in the day across the seeds and half-dead vegetation from the flower shop's back room. Hungry slurps reached Seymour's ears through his grunts. The plant gulped his batter down, but refused to release its lip-lock on his deflating tool. He gave his dick a tug. It popped out of the warm pink mouth. Seymour raised the plant up to eye level.

"Did you like that, little fellow?"

The plant grinned then burped. "Feed me," it said.

Seymour took it home to the dank apartment where he lived with his neurotic invalid father, and fed it twice more before passing out in his room, spent.

"Seymour, don't you forget my prescriptions."

"I know, I know—how could I forget, Dad?" he said on his way out the door, cradling the plant between both arms. "Or be allowed to."

The plant, an exotic pitcher plant from a remote region of the Amazon that had likely come into the flower shop by accident with far less exotic imports, had doubled in size following its latest feeding. Seymour's balls, in response, had shrunk to half what they had been and swung less than normal with his steps.

"You sure are a hungry little guy," he whispered after locking the door.

The plant nuzzled its lips against his arms and rewarded him with a kiss. He noticed it had a milk mustache from his last nutting and gave it a rapid spit bath before skipping down the stairs and out of the tenement, onto the sidewalk.

"I like you, little fellow," Seymour chuckled. "A lot. So much, in fact, that I'm going to call you Austin II. That's right, I'm naming you after the finest, classiest guy I know. You probably seen him at the flower shop before somebody forgot you in the back room. Austin—the real one, I mean—he's mostly a front-of-the-store sort of dude. Head flower arranger. Shit, he can arrange the head of my big pink bouquet any way he wants to, any time."

Seymour chuckled.

"Feed me," Austin II said.

Seymour covered the plant's mouth. "You, you be quiet there, babe. I don't want every Tom, Dick and Harry knowing you can talk. And as for feeding time—you pretty much drained my come-tanks dry. My wang is tuckered out, so you're gonna have to wait awhile until my balls fill up again."

"*Feed me*," Austin II persisted.

Seymour scampered down the sidewalk and eventually reached the flower shop. Inside, Mister Voshnik was pulling at what remained of his grizzled hair and bemoaning his fate. Beautiful Austin hummed a happy tune in counterpoint behind his crafting table, where he danced in place arranging lush irises as purple as Seymour imagined his dick now looked.

"And there he is, late again," Mister Voshnik roared.

Seymour checked the clock above the cash register. "Only by three minutes, but I stayed last night for three full hours after my shift, Mister V."

"Don't you Mister V. me. Time is money, Mister Kilkenny— so don't mince with me about your time when it's my money at stake." Voshnik's eyes zeroed in on the plant. "And what is this weed you have with you?"

Seymour straightened. "This is no weed; he's a really amazing plant unlike any other I've ever seen. I thought he would bring extra foot traffic into the store if we displayed him in the window."

"Window displays? Now, suddenly, we're Tiffany's? Where did you get that thing?"

Seymour proudly caressed the area on Austin II's mouth that was cheek on Austin, the Original. "I guess you could say that I created him."

Austin I scooted out from behind his table and glided over. "Oh, Seymour, what an adorable plant. Venus flytrap, is it?"

Penis, more likely, thought Seymour. He chuckled nervously in response. "Something like that."

"He's so cute," Austin continued, gently tickling the plant's lips, under the chin. Austin II cooed.

Seymour licked his lips, unable to stem the vision of Austin's delicate fingers doing the same thing to him, under his nut sac. "I'm glad you think so, Austin, because I named him after you. Austin I, meet Austin II. Austin II, meet the famous and incredible Austin I."

Austin smiled, and Seymour melted. Mister Voshnik bellowed a rosary of expletives and clutched at his heart. "You're going to put me in a box, people. Get back to work, would you? Or *start*, for Caesar's sake."

"Yes, Mister Voshnik," Austin I said.

"And you, put that weed in the window. Anything to get the cash flowing again in this sad petal trade that has cursed me, body and soul!"

Seymour cleared a neat place for Austin II among the silk flowers and a ceramic bowl filled with decorative bulbs made from grapevine which, to Seymour, had always reminded him of a plate full of hairy balls, especially given the curly tendrils. But after returning from deliveries later that day, he found Austin II looking in a sadder state than when he'd first discovered him in the alley.

"*Feed...me...*" the plant said when Seymour scooped him into his arms.

Seymour hurried into the back room in time to see Mister Voshnik packing up for the night. "That weed again," the other man huffed, oblivious to the sad state of the plant in his arms. "Lock up for the night when you're done playing tree doctor. Or don't. I'd be better off if vandals robbed the place. At least the insurance would pay me enough to see the world."

Seymour waited. The moment he heard the telltale jingle of bells from the closing front door, he fumbled out his cock and stuck it, limp, between Austin II's pallid pink lips. After ejaculating so much seed the previous night, he struggled to get hard. Austin II was dying and needed a man's batter. That kind of pressure didn't help.

The thump of the bad cover band playing next door at Club Core Man reached him through the silence and his desperate attempts to bone up.

"*Fruit,*" Seymour said.

Picking up Austin II, he pushed through the back door and wandered into the alley.

The rush of warm air was ripe with colliding colognes, sweat and the narcotic smell of summer. Seymour made out numerous bodies moving around in the poor light, some lined against walls, others strutting up and down the alley, presumably taking stock, all of them male. Seymour snuck around the dumpster. The closest man to him, he saw, wore a crisp white shirt, a thin black tie, and a black suit. The handsome face belonged to Wilberforce.

"Hey, dude," Seymour whispered.

Wilberforce glanced up and gave his crotch a squeeze. "'Sup, buddy?"

Seymour waved. "Come here."

Wilberforce uncrossed his big feet and wandered over. Even in the dull light, Seymour could see that Wilberforce was boned up in his dress pants. "Can't stay long. Expecting my usual sucky-sucky from my good pal, Gravis. I like to feed him early, before all those other studs waiting to nut outside the club fill him up too much. That way, I get home to the wife early, and he gets a decent bellyful. I shoot *big*, not that I like to brag."

Perfect, thought Seymour. "Let me do it," he blurted out.

"Let you do what?"

"You know, *sucky-sucky.*" Willing his free hand into motion, he boldly reached out and squeezed Wilberforce's package. Oh yeah, the dude was hard.

"Whoa, pal, I never figured an All-American jock like you would be into sucking dick. And I got to admit, I really like the feminine ones, like Gravis. The ones who look and act like ladies. Well, *look* like them, at least. As for acting, you don't want them being too ladylike back here in the hottest cruising spot in Skid Row, if you know what I mean."

Chuckling, Wilberforce offered a high-five. Instead of meeting it, Seymour dropped to his knees.

"Please, I promise it will be the best hummer of your life."

Wilberforce postured. "What's that thing you're holding?"

"A houseplant."

"Kinky. Oh, what the hell. Gravis must have some other married dude's root down his snack-hole by now. Or several."

Wilberforce unzipped, freeing his dick from imprisonment, along with a set of hairy stones that matched Seymour's on an ordinary day. The musky scent of a real man's crotch filled his next breath.

"Good. Just one thing—I'm sort of shy. You mind closing your eyes?"

"Not at all. We straight dudes do that anyway when we sell ourselves on the illusion that a hole's just a hole. Right now, your mouth looks a lot like Angelina's in the dark, dude."

Wilberforce closed his eyes. Seymour lined up Austin II, who clamped desperately onto the other man's straining cock.

"Fuckin-A, dude. You've done this before, haven't you?" Wilberforce asked.

Seymour mumbled something, telegraphing an affirmative. Austin II sucked.

Two hours later, after the plant guzzled three full loads, Wilberforce staggered out of the alley, soaked in sweat, a ridiculous grin on his face.

Nourished on a steady diet of anonymous spunk, Austin II quickly outgrew the window display at the front of Voshnik's Flower Shop. Seymour moved him into the emptied back room, where the exotic pink plant, cousin to the Giant Pitcher, the Corpse Flower, and the Mega-Venus Flytrap, drew daily throngs of customers and the curious into the store.

"Seymour, my boy, you've done it," Mister Voshnik said, throwing his arms around him, an awkward dance coordinated to the endless melody of the front door's jingle bells counterpointed by the cash register in constant motion. "I'm making almost as much as I would if we got robbed, and only slightly less than if we set the place on fire and collected the insurance. If this keeps up, we can open a satellite flower shop in Beverly Hills. All because of you—and Austin II. My good boy, I'm giving you a raise."

Seymour blushed. "Golly, Mister Voshnik, you don't need to do that."

"No, I insist. And a significant one—a whole quarter more an hour."

"Wow," Seymour said, smiling widely. "Mister Voshnik, thanks!"

More customers streamed in to gape at Austin II, who now stood a commanding ten feet tall in height. His massive pink flower, leaves and vines stretched nearly as wide.

Voshnik scurried over to the register, relieving Austin I, who had chipped a nail on the keys. The magnificent creature glided back over to Seymour and wrapped an arm around his shoulder. Seymour tensed.

"I'm so proud of you, sugar," Austin said.

Seymour choked down a heavy swallow, aware that he'd gotten hard. "Gee, Austin, it wasn't nothing."

"Oh, but it was, Seymour. Dear, handsome Seymour."

Austin ran a finger along his ear, under his baseball cap. Seymour shuddered. "Austin?"

"With that raise, you can afford to take me out properly."

Seymour's cheeks flushed. "You mean that, Austin? Really?"

"I do."

Seymour took Austin I in his arms, no longer embarrassed by the obvious tent in his jeans or the expanding circle of wetness—precome that would have been meant for one Austin but was now apparently going to the other. He crushed his mouth over Austin's and was rewarded by a playful poke of tongue.

Austin II quietly observed.

"You're going to have to move to Beverly Hills, Voshnik," one of the customers said. "With all those holes in the wall behind that monstrous plant, this place is going to come tumbling down on top of you if you don't!"

Seymour broke contact with Austin's lips and coughed. Luckily, the lure of a different kind of green distracted Voshnik from the telling comment.

Night fell, and men cruised around in the alley.

"*Feed me*," a deep male voice commanded on the other side of the new glory holes Seymour had drilled into the brick wall, behind the dumpster.

Several at a time, dudes poneyed up, slid their cocks into the wet mouth waiting on the other side, and the suckees gave the sucker what he needed.

STALL WALLS

Shane Allison

OMFG, that's him! The twink I sucked off in the bath-room at Tom Brown Park last week. Fuck is he doing in the mall? Damn, he's even cuter outside the piss-pungent bath-rooms. The light sucks in those shitters. I can barely see the dick I'm sucking in front of my face. That's definitely him. I can tell 'cause of the tattoo on his hand. So he's a boarder? Skater punks are totally my type—'specially raggedy freckled-faced redheads. This guy's gotta huge dick. He's got one of those Prince Alberts that hang from the head of it. Look at him eating that eggroll. Fuck, he's got sexy lips. I love white dudes with sexy lips. He's such a tease though, the type that knows he's got it like that. He had my mouth watering for his street meat for weeks, before he finally let me have it under the stall. I didn't waste any time throwing my lips to it. Dick tasted salty and sweaty. I sucked it like it was the last one on earth. I was surprised that he was into me. Guys don't make passes at guys with fat asses.

He took me by the head and skull-fucked the hell out of me.

When he came, he left me there on the floor of the stall hawking his jizz in yellow toilet water, but with a prick like his, it was well fucking worth it. Tom Brown Park is just one of the hot spots I frequent. This mall is another one. I'm not trying to make this shit a habit though. I already got arrested once this year for showing my dick to the wrong guy, who turned out to be an undercover cop. But what else is there? Where else can we go? Wouldn't be no problems if Tallahassee had like a bathhouse or something. For a college town though, there's never a shortage of dick to be had. These guys from a couple of the frat houses on campus keep me swimmin' in men.

He's acting like he don't see me. I should go over and say hey, but I don't want to freak him out. Damn, he got a pretty dick. Thing curls up like a banana. I was surprised he was able to get it through the glory hole. Took him forever to come, not that I'm complaining. I don't know nothing about sk8ter boys other than that crazy shit I've seen on "Scarred." That shit's crazy. Dudes be breaking they legs, arms, wrists, damn ankle bones. This one guy was trying to skate off the handrailing of some steps, and he landed right on his balls. He had all this blood in his jeans. The doctor had to reattach one of them. I had to cross my legs over seeing something that fucked up.

I betcha he's got a girlfriend. A hot piece of ass like him? I can tell he's one of these guys on the down low. I bet his booty is just as freckled as his face, all that red fur around a tight asshole. I would crawl through a ditch of shit and snot to find out. He types away on his laptop between forking brown rice into his mouth. I'm saving up for one. Till then, I'm using the crap-ass computers at the public library. I should have just nutted up and bought one with my financial aid money.

Fuck, he's fixing to go. He throws away what's left of his Chinese food, packs up his PC, picks up his board and holds

it close against his right hip. Oh, shit, he's walking toward the
food court bathrooms. Hell yeah, that's what's up! I get up and
follow him down the hollow hall, past the pay phones. He turns
and looks dead at me. I could never be a private investigator. I
would be so crappy at it. When I think about his dick behind
those brown, tattered shorts, mine starts to rise in my jeans,
twitching in denim and aching to get out. My heart is racing.
I can feel the adrenaline in me start to bubble up. I'm dead on
his heels. Or should I say...Vans. My palms are sweaty. I'm so
horny. I want to suck some dick. I want to suck *his* dick. The
hinges of the door scream as I push it open. "Oh, sorry," I say
to this older dude who I almost hit in the face. All the stalls are
occupied. The bathroom reeks. He's standing up to the urinal.
The bag with his lappy inside hangs off his left shoulder. He
leans his board against the side of the urinal. I saunter up to
the one next to him, undo my jeans, hook my finger over the
elastic of my Fruit of the Looms, and pull my dick out. I don't
gotta pee. The two of us just stand there like we don't know
each other. I stare down at a chewed piece of green gum at the
bottom of yellow water. I wonder about the stray blond pube
hairs on the lip of the urinal, whether they belong to some hot
golden-haired man. I'm so nasty.

He smells like dirt and bubblegum. I look over peripherally
at his dick. It's just as hung and huge as I remember. My cock is
average, but I'm happy with it. Old dudes love it up their asses.
Look at all that pretty strawberry-red crotch fur. I wanna just
knead my face in it, sniff it, feel them coarse on my tongue. He's
stroking his dick. His fingernails are painted death-metal-black.
I can't see much of the tat on his hand because the sleeve from
his hoodie covers most of it. I can feel his eyes on me as I start
to play with mine.

His prick is nicer. I move over closer until our arms graze.

The roar of toilet water startles me. I'm a little nervous, scared of mall cops. Two men exit out of their stalls. I watch them over his shoulder washing their hands. They look at each other in the mirror as if they've been up to something dirty. I'm happy to see them leave so this sk8ter stud and I can be alone. I slowly reach over and take his dick in my hand. I squeeze it. It's so warm and hard. I play with the piercing in the head. When he touches mine, butterflies rustle up in my gut, dirty white fingers around my black piece. I yank my underwear down some more. I want to show him my balls. My eyes don't leave his dick and his don't leave mine either. I'm about to get on my knees when someone walks in. Fuck! We quickly yank our hands away. That's the only thing I hate about this tearoom—the food court traffic. The guy is dressed nerdy. He works as a clerk at Walden Books. He stands at one of the pissers farther down from us. We keep playing with our dicks to keep them hard. A pearl of precum hangs off the ring that runs through the hot-pink head of his cock. The sk8ter boy, I mean, not the nerdy guy. The *bookish* clerk lets out a few farts as he pees. He's oblivious to what we are doing. Straight boys are like that. He flushes, zips up and leaves without washing.

We take up where we left off. It's so risky. I can't get caught. This mall has a trespassing warning against me. "Let's go in the stalls." I whisper. He grabs his board and takes the larger one at the end of the bathroom. I take the one next to him. I latch the door closed. Splotches of piss stain the rim of my toilet. I roll off some tissue and dry it clean before I take down my baggy denim shorts and plop down on the commode. I can hear him rustling with his stuff. He rests his board in a corner of his stall. I like the design of Chinese dragons and Ying Yangs. My dick keeps erect 'cause of what's about to go down. I smear precum along its thick head. I glide my hand under his stall signaling him to stick his dick under. He drops to his knees. Look at that juicy cock! This guy rules! The tats on his legs really stand out against his rice-white skin.

I slide off of my toilet to turn and face him. I stretch my heavyset body till it aches. I can only get the pierced crown past these lips. He pushes under farther. I want the whole thing in my mouth. My neck starts to hurt. The muscles in my legs begin to ache. I'm so out of shape. "Come over here," he tells me as he caresses the back of my head. I can hear someone walking down the hall outside the bathroom that doesn't provide much recovery time. When the door opens, we haul up off our knees and sit back on our toilets. Please don't let it be a cop. He's not thankfully. We wait quietly as this guy pisses. I pray that the young boarder doesn't get scared and leave. He's the first piece of hot ass I've had in weeks.

This one doesn't bother to wash either before he takes off. I pull up my jeans and exit out of my stall. I rap gently on his door. He opens up, his ass bare to me. He unfurls a lengthy piece of tissue from the dispenser. He brings the tip of his tongue to the folded end of the ribbon of dainty tissue paper and sticks it against the exposed slit between the partition and the stall door. He flings his shorts off his legs. They land under the sink. He sits back on the toilet, then points his dick toward me like he knows how badly I want it. We take each other's dick in our hands. He brushes his hair out of his face. He moves in to kiss me. I can taste cigarette on his rosy-red lips. His hand leaves my dick when I drop to my knees. I don't hesitate. Fuck, I love dick! I go balls deep, lips encircle it. Devour that shit. The Prince Albert feels funny in my mouth. "Eat my balls," he tells me. I love to be made to do dirty things by dirty boys. His balls hang big. I lick and suck them. The hair on his pouch feels coarse. Dude stops me when he feels me going lower.

"Let me eat your ass."

"No, that's gross," he says.

"C'mon." He resists in the beginning, but soon gives in. He turns around and straddles his toilet, gripping the metal rail that runs along the wall. His ass is fat and pimpled. My brown-skinned mitts juxtapose nicely against his rice-paper-white ass. I gently pry his cheeks apart. Red fur actually does surround it. So pink, fucking tight. Suck my finger, then press my index digit against those asslips. He reaches behind and tries to push my hand away, but he doesn't put up a fuss when I press my tongue tip there, when I bury my face in it licking and snorting, hoggish. He loves my rim job and will want it done to him all the time now. I fold his dick under his balls and suck the head. This punk wants his dick blown. He turns back around to face me. I kneel to him like he's God. Pull my shirt up over my head, behind my neck. He stands over me, dick over my chest, licking those passion-pink lips. "Come on my face."

I open up like a good slut. I drink the precum from the metal ring through his cockhead. Tongue his slit, taste a little piss. He works it back into my mouth where it belongs. As I worship him like a hero, I look up into his emerald-green eyes. He's so fucking rad. I want him to be my boyfriend, my pierced-dicked, redheaded, rad boyfriend. I run my hands up his tattooed thighs, fingers sliding up his back, under his *Good Charlotte* T-shirt. His body's warm. If only I had a place. It's so risky in here. I'm not seventeen anymore. I could get jail time this time.

He holds my head down on it as he begins to thrust. My throat is numb from the Anbesol I applied, so as not to gag. He punches my throat. I hold on to his ass as he uses me.

"Suck that cock, nigger." He remembered that I like to be called that. His thrusts quicken. He's about to shoot. I can feel it. I hug his big sk8ter cock hard with my lips. I claw his butt.

I'm pouring with sweat. Fuck my face!

"I'm 'bout to...Jes...!" I take my mouth off his dick seconds before he skeets on my face and glasses. I shut my eyes. I can feel it dripping off my nose onto my lips. Cum tastes salty. I take what's left and slather it onto my own cock. I watch him through spunk-stained frames getting dressed. I want him to see me come, but like the rest of these assholes out here, he's in a hurry to get away from me out of the stall, out of the bathroom. He grabs his skateboard, the bag with his lappy in it, and throws the strap over his head and onto his shoulder. He undoes the latch of the stall door and hauls ass leaving me there as if he never knew me. I shoot off, cum oozes over my fingers onto the frigid floor. I grab a few tissues to clean his cum from my face, glasses and hands. I pull my shirt from around my neck back over my head. I can barely get up. I'm so out of shape. I could get more guys if I lost some weight. I wash my hands, check myself in the mirror and exit out into the hall that smells of chicken teriyaki. I drive home with his cum dry on my lips knowing I will see him again. I always do.

ABOUT THE
AUTHORS

JONATHAN ASCHE'S stories have appeared in numerous magazines as well as many anthologies, including *Muscle Men*, *Brief Encounters* and *Best Gay Erotica 2011*. He has written two erotic novels and the collection *Kept Men and Other Erotic Stories*. He lives in Atlanta with his husband, Tomé.

BEARMUFFIN'S stories appeared in many of the gay porn magazines that were popular from the '80s through the '00s. These days his work can be found in anthologies by Cleis Press, STARbooks Press and Bold Strokes Books. He lives in San Diego, California and loves to travel in search of grist for his literary mill.

DANIEL CURZON is the author of the first gay protest novel, *Something You Do in the Dark* (1971) and many other novels. His *Godot Arrives* won the 1999 National New Play Contest.

RYAN FIELD has worked in publishing for the past twenty years as an editor, journalist and writer. He's the author of the best-selling *Virgin Billionaire* series and his *An Officer and a Gentleman* was recently released by Alyson Books in print, in collaboration with ravenousromance.com. He blogs at ryanfield.blogspot.com.

SHAUN LEVIN is the author of *Snapshots of The Boy* and *A Year of Two Summers*. He is the editor of *Chroma: A Queer Literary and Arts Journal*.

JEFF MANN has published two books of poetry, *Bones Washed with Wine* and *On the Tongue*; a collection of memoir and poetry, *Loving Mountains, Loving Men*; a book of essays, *Edge*; and a volume of short fiction, *A History of Barbed Wire*, winner of a Lambda Literary Award.

BOB MASTERS has had work appear in the *James White Review* and *RFD*. He writes short stories and poetry and is currently hard at work on his very first novel.

GREGORY L. NORRIS writes regularly for national magazines and fiction anthologies. He is the author of the handbook to all-things-Sunnydale, *The Q Guide to Buffy the Vampire Slayer*. Norris lives and writes at the outer limits of New Hampshire.

DONALD PEEBLES JR. is a lifelong resident of Jamaica, New York. He is an author, writer, blogger and poet who has been published in *Urban Dialogue, Shoutout!, SBC, Writes of Passage USA* and *Flesh to Flesh*. He is working on two novels, *Hooker Heritage* and *Bastards and Bitches*.

ROB ROSEN, author of *Sparkle: The Queerest Book You'll Ever Love* and *Divas Las Vegas,* has contributed to more than one hundred anthologies. Please visit him at therobrosen.com.

AARON TRAVIS's first erotic story appeared in 1979 in *Drummer Magazine.* Over the next fifteen years he wrote dozens of short stories, the serialized novel *Slaves of the Empire* and hundreds of book and video reviews. His web page is stevensaylor.com/AaronTravis/.

BOB VICKERY has had five collections of stories published: *Skin Deep, Cock Tales, Cocksure, Play Buddies,* and most recently, *Man Jack,* an audio-book of some of his hottest stories. Bob lives in San Francisco and can most often be found in his neighborhood Haight Ashbury café, pounding out the smut on his laptop.

Approximately fifty of **MARK WILDYR's** short stories and novellas exploring developing sexual awareness and intercultural relationships have been acquired by such publishers as *Freshmen* and *Men's* Magazines, Alyson, Arsenal Press, Cleis and STARbooks Press. *Cut Hand,* his full-length historical novel, was published in June of this year. His website is markwildyr.com.

CHUCK WILLMAN has had several erotic stories and essays published in *FirstHand, Manscape* and *Guys* magazines. He currently lives in Las Vegas with his partner of twenty-two years and loves hanging out naked in the desert.

JEREMY ANDREWS WINDSOR is the *nom de plume* (since he holds a BA in French) of a writer living in Washington, DC.

Under his real name, he has published several short stores, and his first novel is upcoming from MLR Press.

GERARD WOZEK's first book of poetry, *Dervish*, won the Gival Press Poetry Award. His most recent book is a collection of short fiction and travel tales, *Postcards from Heartthrob Town*.

ABOUT
THE EDITOR

SHANE ALLISON is the editor of *Hot Cops, Firemen, Hard Working Men, College Boys, Brief Encounters, Afternoon Pleasures: Erotic Stories for Gay Couples,* and *Frat Boys.* His first collection of poetry, *Slut Machine,* is out from Queer Mojo Press. He is at work on a new collection of poetry as well as more hot new gay erotic anthologies.

More from Shane Allison

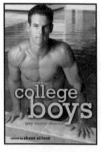

Ordering is easy! Call us toll free or fax us to place your MC/VISA order.
You can also mail the order form below with payment to:
Cleis Press, 2246 Sixth St., Berkeley, CA 94710.

ORDER FORM

QTY	TITLE	PRICE
————	————————————————————————	————
————	————————————————————————	————
————	————————————————————————	————
————	————————————————————————	————
————	————————————————————————	————
————	————————————————————————	————
————	————————————————————————	————
————	————————————————————————	————

SUBTOTAL ————

SHIPPING ————

SALES TAX ————

TOTAL ————

Add $3.95 postage/handling for the first book ordered and $1.00 for each additional book. Outside North America, please contact us for shipping rates. California residents add 8.75% sales tax. Payment in U.S. dollars only.

★ Free book of equal or lesser value. Shipping and applicable sales tax extra.

Cleis Press • Phone: (800) 780-2279 • Fax: (510) 845-8001
orders@cleispress.com • www.cleispress.com
You'll find more great books on our website

Follow us on Twitter @cleispress • Friend/fan us on Facebook